BALLANTINE BOOKS • NEW YORK

A Del Rey Book
Published by Ballantine Books

Library of Congress Catalog Card Number: 61-14968

ISBN 0-345-27119-X

This edition published by arrangement with Holt, Rinehart and Winston

Manufactured in the United States of America

First Ballantine Books Edition: November 1977

Cover art by Dean Ellis

BACKLASH

The broken strut whipped against the side of the girl's spacesuit, ripping a gash a foot long. Air rushed out. She grabbed at the cut, her face horrified, as the pressure sank.

Fred leaped forward and caught her. She had only minutes of air left.

The tractor was the only possible place to take her. So Fred slung her over his shoulder and ran.

The outer lock was open. He leaped inside, still carrying the girl, and snapped it shut. Then he forced his way through the inner lock. It gave suddenly, and they crashed through. The force of his thrust slammed him against the control panel at the front of the cabin.

Abruptly, the little tractor seemed to sag under him; the nose dipped, and the machine began to slip.

Fred scarcely had time to realize that the tractor was falling over the edge of the cliff before it began hurtling to the pit floor sixty feet below . . .

Also by Lester del Rey
published by Ballantine Books:

NERVES
THE ELEVENTH COMMANDMENT
STORIES FROM AND SOME WERE HUMAN
POLICE YOUR PLANET (with Erik van Lhin)
GODS AND GOLEMS
THE EARLY DEL REY (in 2 volumes)
MORTALS AND MONSTERS
ROBOTS AND CHANGELINGS
FANTASTIC SCIENCE FICTION ART 1926-1954

To Paul Waterman

Contents

CHAPTER 1 /

Emergency Action

AS FRED HALPERN trotted onto the rocket field, the sun was setting. Long shadows lanced from the little high-jump ships toward the east, where the pale Moon was already visible. It should have been a beautiful sight to a rocketman, but Fred scarcely noticed it. Instead, he glanced in worry at the watch strapped outside his suit and quickened his pace. The spacesuit jounced awkwardly on his lean, medium-height body; under his helmet, his black hair was plastered down by perspiration, and there was a frown on his thin face.

This was Elimination Week at Goddard Space Academy, and it was no time to be late for an assignment. Normally, the delay while he replaced a cracked helmet might be enough excuse, but not this week. Out of sixty cadets in the class, at least forty were to be washed out. The Academy instructors were deliberately trying every trick they could imagine to make the students fail. Only the ones who couldn't be eliminated were considered good enough to graduate into careers in space.

The minute hand was almost touching the hour mark as Fred pounded up to the little ship assigned to him. Beside the ship, an instructor stood waiting, also studying a watch. The man's slow nod assured Fred that he wasn't late, and he began to breathe more easily as he halted and came to salute. Then, at the sight of the face under the raised helmet visor, he stiffened again.

"Well, well. So I draw the Moon-boy?" Major Wickman's voice seemed contemptuously amused. He was tall and heavily built for a pilot, with a round face that could be attractive when he smiled. He wasn't smiling now; his blond mustache was lifted in a faint sneer. "Haven't they washed you out yet, Moon-boy?"

"No, sir," Fred told him carefully, struggling to keep the anger from his voice.

Wickman grinned. "Then we'll have to do something about that sorry situation. All right, Mr. Halpern, get on board! We can't wait for your reporter friends this time."

Fred felt his face reddening, and turned hastily to the little ladder leading up to the ship's entrance. The painful part of what Wickman had said was that there was some truth in it.

Four years before, Fred Halpern had made a complete fool of himself, as he realized now. He had managed to take off from the Space Station in a small rocketship and reach the Moon before the other ships were ready to go. As a result, the whole Moon expedition was forced to take off ahead of schedule to rescue him, at the cost of one man's life. It had been a completely foolish stunt, but it made wonderful newspaper copy, turning him into something of a hero on Earth. Even now, the reporters considered him a good news subject. When he'd been disciplined by Wickman for breaking a minor rule of the Academy, the reporters had made him a martyr and pictured Wickman as a bullying martinet. Apparently, the instructor still resented it bitterly.

Silently they drew up the ladder and dogged the little entry port shut. Fred dropped into the student seat in the tiny cabin, staring out through the portholes, while Wickman opened the envelope containing instructions, glanced through them, and passed one sheet to Fred.

Surprisingly, the assignment looked like a routine one. The little high-jump ships were powered with a new fuel that permitted them to take off and rise into close orbit around the Earth without the booster stages. This seemed to be just such a single maneuver; they were to climb three hundred miles above the surface, swing into orbit, circle the Earth once, and land back on the field, braking down on the stubby wings of the ship. It was *too* simple, Fred thought; something must be arranged to go wrong somewhere to offer a tougher test of his ability. But he could find no evidence of it in his instructions.

"Worried, Moon-boy?" Wickman asked. When Fred made no answer, his voice sharpened. "I asked you a question, Mr. Halpern!"

"Sorry, sir. No, I'm not worried."

"That's right. I keep forgetting you're a hero." Wickman chuckled softly. "You never worry, of course. But maybe you should this time."

Fred felt himself tightening, then forced himself to relax. Wickman might be trying to make him nervous and force him to react badly to the emergency that must be planned somewhere on this flight. He noticed the instructor hadn't turned on the little recorder that kept a record of everything during the flight until after he finished speaking. It was against the rules for an instructor to act in such a manner, of course, but Fred could never prove it afterward.

He checked off his figures on the small course computer that lay between the two control panels, and the results confirmed what he had known already. He seemed to have a gift for analyzing orbits accurately in his head, but this time he needed the reassurance of the computer. Then he began checking the ship, studying his dials as the readings came in.

When he finished, Wickman moved the large selector lever between the controls from "Instructor" to "Student." The little ships were designed to operate from either of two sets of independent controls, and all the dials read in duplicate. This setting placed full control of the ship in Fred's circuit.

"Take over, Mr. Halpern!" Wickman ordered.

"Taking over, sir," Fred acknowledged. He flipped on the radio and reached for the microphone. "Flight thirteen to tower."

The tower operator seemed bored. "Tower to thirteen. You're all cleared for circumpolar orbit. Take off at six fifteen."

About a minute later, the chronometer on the panel indicated the quarter-hour, and Fred punched down the firing key. There was no warming-up period in these ships. The monopropellant fuel needed no separate oxidizer or mixing. It was pumped from the tank through the injector nozzle, struck a mesh of heavy copper, and instantly burst into explosion. Fire sprayed out of the rockets against the concrete pad, lighting up the whole landscape, and the little ship shot upward on its savage jet of flame.

The pressure of two gravities of acceleration added to the normal single gravity pull of Earth to drive Fred back sharply against the seat. Every cell of his body seemed to weigh three times what it should, and his hands felt stiff and clumsy on the controls. But he was used to heavier thrusts than this, and he began making the tiny corrections needed to hold the course precisely accurate. He could have depended on automatic controls and made his corrections afterward, but that wasted fuel, and his final mark would depend on efficiency as well as accuracy in his piloting.

Twenty seconds after take-off, they reached supersonic speed. There was a faint shaking, but the ship took the change smoothly at the two miles of height and went on climbing.

A minute after take-off, at a height of twenty miles where the air was thin and offered lower resistance, Fred pulled the fuel lever back. Now their rate of acceleration doubled, and five times normal weight pressed him back into the seat. His lungs fought for breath, his arms felt like lead against the supports that held them, and even his fingers were hard to control. There was less than three minutes of such acceleration.

During the brief "high gravity" period, the ship had turned in answer to his feeble actions. It was now heading around the Earth toward the North Pole, rising slowly toward orbit at three hundred miles up, and traveling at more than five miles a second. Now, at a flip of his finger, the rockets shut off and they coasted along on momentum.

Without the thrust of the rockets, there was no feeling of weight. The pull of Earth was acting on the ship and the men's bodies to slow them and force them into an elliptical orbit, but the effect of this gravity was exactly counterbalanced by the outward thrust of their inertia. Fred heaved a sigh of relief. He was familiar with the weightlessness of free fall and he liked the feeling. The straps on his seat held him loosely in place as he checked his instruments and ran a test against the radio beacons from Earth. His piloting had been perfect, and they were on course.

"Well done, Mr. Halpern," Wickman commented. The words and his voice were officially correct, obviously meant for the recorder that was taping everything. Fred drew no encouragement from the commendation; the instructor's expression was still amused, as if his orders gave him some secret knowledge of what was to come.

No trouble seemed to develop, however. They passed over the North Pole beacon and received official acknowledgment of the accuracy of their course. At the top of their orbit, Fred made a single corrective blast to change their elliptical flight into a true circle around Earth, and they cruised on without further need to do anything.

Ahead of him and much higher, he now could make out the bright speck of the big manned satellite in its permanent orbit. Stanley Station was where he had received his first experience in space as a boy. His father was still in command of it, probably too busy outfitting the latest Moon expedition to notice the little high-jump ship so far below.

In its higher orbit, the big station was traveling more slowly, and Fred began to catch up to it, then passed under it. It was far behind him when he neared the South Pole.

Here more correction was needed, since the Earth was turning eastward under them. If they continued in a true circle, Goddard Academy would be far to the east of them by the time they landed. It was also time to begin dropping back slowly, to make their approach to the braking orbit for landing.

He had already worked out the maneuver in his head and was setting up the controls, but he ran the problem through the computer to be officially correct. The results agreed with his own estimate. The gyroscopes whined faintly as they began twisting the ship around to the proper direction, then stopped. Fred depressed the firing keys briefly for a single blast. Once again, the ship behaved perfectly, setting them on the new course.

"Excellent, Mr. Halpern," Wickman commented.

"Thank you, sir," Fred answered properly. But he was frowning now, more certain than ever that something had to go wrong before they landed. There was no point to testing him with such a routine maneuver during Elimination Week. After his experience in handling the little taxi rocket around Stanley Station, he could have operated any ship in such a maneuver before he ever came to Goddard Space Academy. Even without such experience, his three years at the Academy would have qualified him for routine flights without trouble.

He rechecked his fuel supply, pump and control mechanism, and retested everything he could, but the ship was in top-flight order. Then he studied his instructions again. The landing orbit was unusual, but not difficult. He was to come in very high and lose speed by spiraling down, rather than use the normal direct approach that let atmospheric friction kill his speed. It was needlessly elaborate this way, but nothing he couldn't handle. And still he felt himself tensing up and waiting for trouble.

Nothing happened. The ship came down, finally touching the so-called top of the atmosphere where air resistance began to slow the ship and heat its outer hull. Here the ship could be handled like a glider and the problem was to keep the glide path flat enough to avoid too much heating and still make full use of the constantly denser air to reduce their speed. The complicated little air-cooling units came on, dissipating the heat that leaked through the hull. Everything seemed normal. They moved down to fifty miles high before he began spiraling over the shadow below that was the finger of Florida. Then they were at forty miles, and the radio beacon was checking the course. Fred called the tower for clearance and got routine assurance. Slowly, their speed and height dropped, until they were only thirty miles up, the wings biting firmly into the thin air.

The field below was dark, marked only by lights that were faint dots at this height. Suddenly there was a brighter light—a streak that could only be another little ship taking off. Tower should have notified him, of course, but he had expected to find others taking off. A great many of the test assignments were run at night. He estimated the approach against the other ship's vertical take-off and found that there was more than adequate margin of safety.

Another streak appeared close to the first, indicating a second take-off below. They were apparently running doubles, always tricky, but he still had a margin of safety.

It was Wickman's stare that gave him a scant second's warning. The instructor was watching the take-offs too intently, as if expecting something to happen. Fred's eyes went from the controls to the ports, in time to see the second ship below tilting far too soon, the streak of its exhaust bent sideways, heading toward the area of his own approach.

He saw Wickman's fingers dancing over the course-plotting radar controls just as he reached for his own. The strange, intuitive gift in his mind had already told him it would be close, but that a very slight correction to a steeper descent would put him out of all possible danger. By the rules, a landing rocket must take all corrective action, since the take-off maneuver was much harder to change. If the other pilot should panic, he would probably react toward upward evasion, and thus no harm would be done.

Wickman had swung from the radar to the computer, and he was now tearing off the taped answer. Fred could see only part of the answer Wickman held, but it was wrong. The symbols were for ascent over the other ship, which could mean a collision that would wreck both of them.

"Mr. Halpern, lift . . ." Wickman began.

"I'm going under them, sir," Fred told him sharply.

"I order you up! Course . . ."

Fred's lips tightened, but he shook his head before the other could finish. "I must refuse, sir."

Wickman's hand flipped the selector lever to "Instructor," and his other hand was already on the controls of his board. He was grimacing.

Fred brought his fist down on the lever, snapping it back with a force that broke off the handle and sent a stab of pain up his arm. The delay had brought the two ships closer; there was no time to check his course. He pushed the flight lever forward, risking as sharp a dip as he dared. He heard the servo-motors on the elevator controls groan, and the ship bucked. But its descent steepened sharply. Almost at once, the hull temperature indicator began moving into the red danger zone, but Fred held his course as long as he dared, before leveling off.

The rising ship went by less than half a mile above

him, but with more than adequate clearance. Now the temperature of the hull was falling. The cooling units inside were laboring, yet the air was still comfortable.

He stole a glance at Wickman. The instructor was staring ahead, not bothering to watch Fred's corrections to bring the ship back into its proper landing course.

The control tower began barking questions. Fred answered them tersely and confirmed his previously calculated landing time. It meant difficult flying to compensate for the sudden descent; however, he was sure of himself now. He flattened his glide as much as he could. They bucked below supersonic speed and began gliding down like a normal plane, heading for the long landing strip. When the ship touched the runway, the chronometer pointed to the exact second called for in the original tower instructions.

It wasn't until they had rolled to a stop that Major Wickman turned to face Fred. His voice was almost a purr.

"Mr. Halpern, consider yourself under arrest! You'll return to your quarters and remain in your dormitory until you receive further orders. I'm charging you with insubordination, refusal to obey orders in an emergency, and endangering my life and the lives of the men on the other ship."

He ripped the recorder out of the locker, sealed its record, and grinned as he looked at Fred again. "Don't bother telling the reporters this time, Moon-boy. They'll hear about your mutiny soon enough," he said, and headed for the exit port, whistling softly.

CHAPTER 2 /

Washed Out

BREAKFAST WAS usually a noisy affair, but this morning the mess hall lay under a pall of gloom. Fred slipped into his seat as the final bell rang, wanting to sink through the floor rather than meet the looks of the other cadets. Under the rules of his house arrest, conversation with him was forbidden, but no rule could stop them from staring at him, either in gloating or pity.

Then the silence in the hall finally registered, and he looked up, unable to avoid the faces any longer. But no one was looking at him. All eyes were centered on the doorway where red-headed Bill Fallon was entering. A group of cadets started toward the big man, but he waved them back, trying to smile. He looked sick.

"No dice," he reported to the room. "They didn't like my final course plotting. I'm washed out, officially."

Fred's own sickness deepened at the news. Fallon had been voted the most popular cadet in the class for three years; even the instructors had liked him. That hadn't helped, though, during the grind of Elimination Week.

Now there was a mumble of unhappy conversation as Fred tried to go on eating. His hand hurt from the bruise where he'd hit the control lever, and he had no idea of what he was eating. He went on mechanically because there was nothing else to do.

It was almost a relief when the speaker in the hall

made the grating sound that always preceded a message.

"Cadet Frederick Halpern will report to the office of the Commandant," it announced.

Now the eyes were centered on him. Fred got up slowly, discovering that his legs would still support him, and started down the aisle toward the door.

A hand reached out for his suddenly, and he looked down in surprise to see that it belonged to Bill Fallon. The cadet had turned to face him with genuine sympathy.

"Good luck," Fallon said. "We'll be rooting for you."

"Thanks. I—I'm sorry about . . ." Fred tried to shape some expression of regret that would sound right, but the words wouldn't come.

Fallon shrugged the attempt aside. "Forget about me, kid. Just keep your chin up and remember you've still got a chance."

Somehow, the words seemed to help a little. Fred braced himself again, marching out of the hall more firmly. Outside, the bright Florida sunshine almost blinded him as he turned down the graveled walk toward the office of Commandant Olson. He began shaping his explanations for the interview. He'd been over them a dozen times already in his mind before getting to sleep, but now he started rehearsing in earnest.

Then all his speeches evaporated into nothing as the girl in the reception room took his name and ushered him directly into the big oak-lined office.

He came to an automatic salute. "Cadet Halpern reporting, sir."

"At ease, Cadet." The heavy face under a shock of iron-gray hair was unsmiling, but it seemed friendly enough. Commandant Olson pointed to a chair beside the big desk. "Take a seat while I finish going over this report on you again. And you might look at the complaint Major Wickman filed."

Fred sank into the chair, taking the paper in fingers that trembled a little. He had to force his eyes to focus on it, and the first sentences seemed to make no sense until he had read them for the third time.

The complaint was short and direct. It gave the simplest possible account of the final events of the test flight and Fred's actions. There was nothing that was untrue; the cold, direct report needed no untruth to make it seem like a hopeless condemnation when Fred's own reasons were omitted. The charge was stated against him, with the recommendation that he be dropped from the Academy as unsuitable for graduation.

Fred was just finishing the report when Major Wickman was ushered into the office, to be waved to a chair on the other side of the desk. The instructor's face was rigidly correct, without a trace of emotion.

The Commandant shoved the last of the papers back into a folder and turned to Fred. "Well, young man, it seems you're in pretty serious trouble. Do you find anything wrong with Major Wickman's report?"

"It's correct, as far as it goes," Fred admitted reluctantly.

Olson tapped the little recorder on his desk. "It seems to agree with the flight tape. What do you think is omitted?"

It wasn't going the way Fred had rehearsed it. He shook his head slowly, aware that he couldn't prove anything about the badgering Wickman had done before the flight. "The report's correct, sir."

Wickman leaned forward, a thin smile on his lips. "I think Mr. Halpern meant that I hadn't included his estimation of the dangers of the maneuver in my report, sir," he suggested. "He seemed to believe he understood the situation better than the computer analysis."

"And what were the results of your computations, Fred?" The Commandant's face broke into a faint smile with the use of the first name, but there was no real reassurance in the gesture.

Fred swallowed before answering. "I—I didn't make a computation."

"You didn't?" Olson's face clouded, and he turned to the tape recorder, rerunning the final part of the tape. "No, I see. I missed that. Then just how did you estimate your course?"

Wickman, Fred decided, had been very clever; he'd managed to bring up new evidence without making it seem like an accusation. This might be more serious than what was already on the report.

Wickman was speaking, making the explanation for him. "Mr. Halpern believes he can estimate orbits and courses in his head, without using a computer. Or so I gather from what I hear from other students. I've heard that such talents do exist—a few billiard experts seem able to sense the factors affecting a complicated curve. And in all fairness, I must admit the course adopted by Mr. Halpern resulted in an excellent landing approach."

"There was no time to use the computer," Fred explained hastily.

"But there was time to determine that the course plotted by Major Wickman was wrong, Fred? Is that what you're saying?"

Fred nodded. "I didn't have to plot it. I could feel it was wrong. You know the rules for take-off maneuvering; the other pilot would have corrected upward, if he did anything. And if he did . . ."

"There's that in your favor, yes," Olson admitted. "I've already considered it. And I suppose you couldn't have known that both other ships were being flown by instructors who were not going to make such a maneuver upward. But without computing a course downward . . ."

He left the sentence incomplete, frowning again. Then he shrugged. "Perhaps you have such a talent as you feel you do. I'll grant that for the moment, though I don't see how it can be proved. And it might not be reliable every time, even so. But . . ."

"I can prove it," Fred interrupted. If he could show them, he might still be able to establish the reason for his action. "If you'll let me take a ship up on any course without a computer, I'll prove it. I'll bring it down on schedule without using more than minimum fuel. I want to prove it, sir."

At once he saw that he'd made a mistake. The smile on Wickman's face twitched slightly, and the frown deepened on the features of the Commandant.

Olson shook his head slowly. "I gather that it's very important to you to prove such an ability? And you'd be willing to risk almost anything to prove it? Is that why you deliberately disobeyed your landing instructions from Major Wickman?" He waited, while Fred tried to find an answer, then asked more sharply, "Is it important to you to prove you can be the only pilot here who doesn't need a computer?"

"I'm not sure it matters how Mr. Halpern lays his course, sir," Wickman suggested. "I must admit that he is without any question the most accomplished pilot I've seen. Perhaps he's better than I am, judging by the accuracy of his course corrections."

Olson chuckled suddenly. "Are you accusing this young man or defending him, Major? I'm quite aware of the fact that his actual flying record is excellent in every way."

"Sorry, sir," Wickman said, his face again without expression.

It was smooth, Fred thought. It was too smooth. Wickman would manage to ruin any defense he might make without actually attacking him. And there was no answer he could find for such tactics.

Olson glanced at him, and then back to some notes. "Umm. Still, I suppose the question really isn't whether he can pilot without a computer. It's the fact that he chose to do so in direct violation of orders, and in a dangerous situation where lives and ships were hanging on his decision. Fred, didn't it occur to you that Major

Wickman might have been acting on more knowledge of the true situation than you had—and that he might have known what the other ships were about to do?"

"No, sir," Fred admitted. "I didn't have time to think of that. And if I had thought of it, I couldn't have risked it."

"You've had a number of demerits for lack of discipline, haven't you?"

Fred nodded. He'd been pretty stupid about discipline when he first came to Goddard. He'd never been used to taking orders; his grandmother raised him during most of his early life, and she'd spoiled him badly. But he'd been trying harder, and most of the past year had gone without trouble over discipline. There'd been the one time with Wickman, but he hadn't really understood his orders that time.

"I don't want to dismiss you," the Commandant was saying, "I really don't, because we need skilled pilots desperately, and because you could be one of our best. But when we put a man in charge of a ship that costs millions of dollars and human lives which are always in danger out in space, that man must be the best we can find. He must be able to think for himself, and he must be able to take discipline whenever it is called for. You've always worried us on that score. In fact, I'll be honest with you—we almost refused your application for admittance here; that business of making a crazy dash for the Moon may have made you a hero to most people, but it worried us. If it hadn't been for the influence of a lot of fine men out there who felt you'd grow out of it, your lack of discipline would have made me reject you. That's why we set up your final test as we did. I asked Major Wickman to suggest . . ."

Surprise and sudden understanding hit Fred then. "Major Wickman, sir?"

"That's right," Olson said. "Major Wickman designed this test for you at my suggestion. It wasn't to test your flying ability. It was simply to see whether you'd obey orders in an emergency. Or whether you'd play a lone hand, disregard superior officers, and make some kind of a play for glory."

"It wasn't a play for glory, sir."

"I'm sure you feel that now. But I've been over your record very thoroughly, Fred. And it worries me. When you first came here, you acted as if you were far superior to the other cadets. You'd had considerable experience in space, and you let them know it. You made quite a few enemies, you know. And you even argued with your instructors. Now, toward the end here, you seem to have improved. But I wonder. Indeed, I wonder. You still aren't popular with the cadets, and that's something I've learned to consider important; maybe they still think you're a 'glory-hog,' as the expression goes. When an emergency arises, you still feel your judgment is better than that of a more trusted pilot. Can you honestly deny there was no desire to show yourself smarter than Major Wickman?"

It hurt; nevertheless Fred couldn't honestly deny it. He'd tried to get over his feeling of being better than the others and the compulsion to be a show-off, but he couldn't really be sure. How could anybody be sure what lay behind all his actions?

"Can Major Wickman deny he's prejudiced against me?" he asked sharply, before he could realize that the words would only make him seem more of a show-off. It wasn't a question to ask about an instructor.

But Wickman nodded. "You're right, Mr. Halpern. I dislike you, and I told Commandant Olson so before the test was assigned to me. I'm definitely prejudiced against you."

"Because I let a couple of reporters know about . . ."

"No!" Wickman interrupted quickly. "Not at all, though that was a lack of respect for the Academy on your part. I disliked you before you ever came here. I disliked you for a fool kid who could risk the lives of all the good men in space, and maybe risk ruining our whole chance to explore the Moon properly. And when you came here I disliked you for acting like a spoiled brat. Space means something to me, Mr. Halpern, and I don't like to see the wrong man get out into space just because his father heads the Station and because he has friends on the Moon."

Fred tried to hold back the anger rising in him, but it was too strong. "If space means so much, why aren't you a real pilot instead of an instructor?"

Commandant Olson leaned forward, and there was no longer any sign of friendliness on his face.

"Major Wickman has remained at the Academy for four years only because I've pleaded with him to stay," he said. "He's here because I need him. He's the best instructor I have. And he's already told me he can't remain any longer and has applied for a piloting berth. I'm sorry to say that I think he may have found a very fine job and be leaving us soon. He's a man who does respect discipline, and you're totally out of order, Mr. Halpern."

"I'm sorry, sir," Fred muttered, but he couldn't face Wickman to make an apology.

Wickman shrugged. "Let it go, sir. The boy is under pressure, and there's his background which should be considered. I take no offense."

There was a moment of silence then, while Olson stared at Fred thoughtfully. Fred braced himself for what the decision must be now. He'd made a complete fool of himself; he'd played squarely into Wickman's hands and confirmed every doubt about his insubordination and lack of discipline.

"Very well," Olson said at last, and there was genuine regret in his voice. "I'm afraid, Mr. Halpern, that I'll have to ask . . ."

The buzzer on the intercom broke into his words, and he flipped up a lever quickly. The receptionist's voice came through tinnily. "There's a call for you from Colonel Halpern on Stanley Station, sir."

Olson glanced quickly at the two others. Then he shrugged. "All right, put it through. And you two might as well stay to hear it, since it probably concerns both of you."

A few seconds later, the face of Fred's father appeared on the tiny screen of the videophone on the desk, relayed from the Station a thousand miles out in space. Olson had the little pickup pointed at himself with the screen turned so the others could see it.

There were brief greetings, and then Colonel Halpern got down to business. To Fred's surprise, it wasn't about the dismissal from the Academy.

"Olson, I've been going over that dossier on the pilot you recommended for our special job, and he looks like the man. But one question. Why do you want to let him go?"

"I don't," the Commandant said. "I can't hold him. Wickman's the best pilot I've had, but after four years, he's itching to get out into real space."

In his chair, Wickman had tensed and leaned forward, a curiously eager look to his whole body.

Olson motioned with his hand to cut off whatever Colonel Halpern was about to say. "Colonel, I'm afraid there's some bad news I'm going to have to break first, though. It's about your son . . ."

Pain lanced across the features on the screen—pain and disappointment—and gave place to a dead, wooden expression. "You're expelling him?"

"We're expelling him," Olson agreed.

Fred's stomach seemed to come up into his throat, and he lost the next few words. Knowing he was to be eliminated and actually hearing it were two different things. Somehow, until that second, some shred of hope had remained.

His father's voice from the speaker broke his shock and brought his mind back into focus. "Did Major

Wickman know he was being considered for special assignment when he preferred charges against my son?"

"He knew, of course," Olson admitted.

Wickman sighed softly, and the expression went out of his eyes, to snap back suddenly at the next words.

"Then convey my respects to him," Colonel Halpern was saying. "I congratulate him on his honesty. Tell him to report here to me on the first ship up. I want to interview him for the assignment before he goes to Ground Command."

"And the boy?" Olson reminded him.

Halpern sighed wearily. "I'll arrange passage on the same ship."

When the screen went dark, the Commandant turned back to the others. "I'll want to talk to you, Major. Fred, I'm sorry, but I couldn't take a chance on you. I really couldn't."

Fred nodded and got up, to go outside and back along the walks, guided by habit, hardly seeing where he was going. On one of the tall poles, a speaker broke into a loud series of orders.

"Attention, all cadets! Attention, all cadets . . ."

He faced sharply toward it. A second later, he choked and turned back to the path, realizing that it no longer applied to him.

He wasn't a cadet. He was washed out.

CHAPTER 3 /

Return to Space

THERE WASN'T much to pack. Most of the things used on Earth were too heavy to ship up to the Station, and the usual weight restrictions limited Fred to fifteen pounds of luggage, including his clothes. He could probably get by with more, since he was Colonel Halpern's son and wouldn't be checked, but he had no desire to break any more rules. Most of his property was piled on the bed, and he pinned a note to it, offering it to any lower classmen who might wander by.

Finally, he stripped off his cadet uniform, taking a long time at it. He folded it neatly and stored it in the closet, before putting on the thin nylon shirt and shorts that were the standard dress for space. The few things he was going to take with him went quickly into a light bag, but he spent a long time checking before he closed it at last.

There was a knock on the door and he jerked around as Bill Fallon came in. The big man glanced around the room in surprise. "All alone?"

"Yeah." There probably had been a party of some kind in Fallon's room before duty called the other cadets away. "Come on in."

Fallon shook his head as he sat down on the loaded bed. "I thought they'd let you stick it out," he said. "I never really expected I could make it, but you're a born pilot."

"They told me I lacked discipline," Fred answered, trying to sound flippant. "Besides, the instructors don't like me either."

Fallon caught the emphasis on the last word and stood up to face the other. "Cut it out, kid. A lot of guys here didn't like you, but a lot did. They got a general assembly call, that's all. My room's been as empty as this one."

It might be true, Fred realized. Some of the cadets might have come to see him off. Then he realized that he didn't deserve the attention. He'd known Fallon was leaving, but he'd forgotten him. Fallon had come to see him, instead. And maybe that was why Fallon was the best-liked guy at the Academy.

"What are you going to do now?" Fred asked him.

Fallon shrugged. "Go back to my father's real estate office, get rich and fat, and forget all this if I can. I dunno. You're lucky. You can get over what they found wrong with you. But I guess I never could learn to use mathematics fast enough to be a pilot, even with Wickman staying up all night to help me."

Fred had no desire to discuss Wickman. He hefted his bag, decided it was light enough, and fastened the little lock. "When are you pulling out?"

"Now. No use hanging around making the other guys feel bad about me. They have troubles enough. I suppose you're going by the main Space Base down the Cape? Maybe we can share a taxi into town, at least."

He went out while Fred gave the room a last look, then came back with a big suitcase in his hand. They went down the steps and out of the hall, heading toward the front gate, where they could call a cab. Neither one could think of anything to say.

The sound of a horn beside them made them stop and turn. It was one of the little staff cars, driven by a first-year cadet. Wickman, who was riding beside the driver, motioned to Fallon. "Want a ride, Bill? I can go right by the station."

"Sure, Sid." Fallon heaved the bag into the back and crawled in beside it. "Come on, kid. This beats having to hire a cab."

Fred shook his head. "No, thanks. I think a walk will do me good."

"Don't be a fool, Moon-boy," Wickman shouted. "We're headed for the same place."

Fred hesitated, hearing Fallon mutter something. Then he shrugged. They wanted discipline and didn't find it while he was here; he'd give it to them on the way out, at least. He climbed in beside Fallon, trying not to notice the chuckle from Wickman.

It was only a few miles to the little town near the Academy, and Fred sat quietly while Wickman and Fallon carried on a lagging conversation. At the bus station, they all got out to shake hands with Fallon and wish him luck—a bitter thing for a man who had just run out of luck, but all they could do. Fred picked up his bag again to head for the local bus that would carry him through the main town and out to the rocket launching field.

As he turned, he heard his name, and a hand grabbed his arm. "Halpern. I thought it was you. What's the idea of the civvies? Hey, wait a minute—you don't mean they busted you out?"

The man was a reporter for the local wire service office. He had interviewed Fred several times before. This time, Fred wanted no story. He pulled away tensely. "No comment," he said, as he'd read of politicians brushing off reporters.

"I'll handle this, Fred." It was Wickman's voice, filled with a warmth and good-fellowship Fred had never heard. "I'll handle this for you."

He watched the Major draw the reporter aside and say something briefly. He stood hesitating about his own course now. Finally he climbed back into the staff car, as Wickman headed back to it.

"Never say 'no comment' to a reporter," the older

man said flatly. "That's what the big shots say when they want to stir up interest. Tell anything—even the truth—to the press, but don't tell them to use their own imagination." Then he laughed. "And don't think I did it for you, Moon-boy. I still don't like false stories being printed about the Academy. So save your thanks."

Fred hadn't meant to thank him. He had his own suspicions about what Wickman might have said, but he kept them to himself. The car swung out on a back road away from the thickly settled area and headed for the rear entrance to the main field. Wickman let him out in front of the largest building.

"See you topside," he said.

Fred muttered a reluctant thanks for the ride and went in to arrange for the flight on which his father would have him booked. Waiting on their launching pads were four of the big multiple-stage rockets. He found none was due to leave until early the next morning, when the Station orbit would lie closer to their normal take-off path. However, there was an official hotel on the field, and a room had been reserved for him.

The room was small, but it had an excellent view of much of the field. Fred glanced out casually, then whistled. He could see the huge rockets far across the field, but something closer held his attention. It was less than a hundred feet high, with fins huge enough to be wings. It looked something like one of the little high-jump rocketships, grown much bigger and fatter. It must be the *Cosmic Egg,* he decided, the first of the real spaceships designed to use the new monopropellant fuel. Supposedly, it could take off from Earth and make the round trip to the Moon, using only a single-stage motor, and carrying more freight than the older ships could carry to the Station.

Fred had read countless articles on the ship in the technical magazines. He hadn't realized it was so nearly completed. Since it had been drawn from the hangar, it must be nearly ready for its first tests.

Those tests must be Wickman's special assignment.

Fred had always dreamed that somehow after graduation he could talk his father into getting him the test pilot's job for the *Cosmic Egg*. It had been the dream of every cadet, but he had felt fairly sure that he could swing it. Now, of course, without any chance for a license, it was impossible for him. And in his place, Wickman would be trying it out.

He started to turn back in disgust, but the beauty of the ship called to him, even if he would never ride in it. This was a ship which could be the turning point in man's exploration of space; with a booster stage added, it might even carry men to Mars or Venus, though its development had come too late for the next Moon expedition. Probably the expedition couldn't have used such a ship, anyhow. The first models of the *Cosmic Egg* would be far too expensive for purchase by this expedition, at least. However there were rumors that three ships already were being built for sale to the World Congress, the international legislative body which had evolved from the old United Nations.

Fred turned away finally and dropped onto the bed. He'd gotten little sleep the night before; the strain and letdown of the day had tired him far more than he expected. He reminded himself that he should have the switchboard call him in the morning, but sleep hit him before he could take care of it.

The room was dark when he wakened, and he saw by the luminous hands of the clock that he'd slept far longer than he'd wanted to. It was still several hours before take-off time. It must have been hunger that wakened him. He bathed and dressed quickly, instinctively reaching for the buttons on what should have been his cadet uniform. With a mutter of disgust at himself, he picked up his bag and went toward the dining room.

One corner of it was open, with a few men sitting at the tables. Wickman was among them, busily talking to a man in the uniform of a co-pilot. Fred found a table some distance away, barely nodding at Wickman's grin. Then he busied himself giving an order for a steak to the bored waitress. Once he got back into space, he'd have no chance to eat good food again. The hydroponic gardens on the Station provided some fresh food and kept the air breathable, but most of the standard diet came from dehydrated meats and vegetables. Such food was edible, but hardly delicious.

The steak wasn't as good as it should have been, either; probably most of the kitchen staff were off for the night. He ate it without complaints. He took time over it, and over a piece of pie. There was nothing else to do until the take-off time arrived.

Wickman passed his table on the way out with the co-pilot. As a fully licensed pilot, naturally Wickman would be permitted aboard ship during the fueling and preliminary checks. Fred might have obtained the same privileges because his father was the head of the Station, but Colonel Halpern frowned on his taking advantage of such position.

"Paper, Moon-boy?" Wickman asked. He was carrying a folded copy of the local Cape paper. Before Fred could reply, he dropped it onto the table and went on across the dining room.

Fred stared at the paper, then reached for it. There was more rocket and space news in this edition than usual, he saw—and this paper specialized in space affairs, since so many of its readers worked on some space project.

He'd been out of touch during the last two weeks of getting ready for the Elimination tests, and he was surprised to read that the Moon expedition was already completed and ready for take-off in three days. Unlike the other, earlier expeditions, which had been official United States projects, this one was being financed from the private funds of a group of scientific foundations. There were hints, too, that the funds provided barely enough to pay for the trip. Shipping even thirty men and supplies across space to the Moon and back was a tremendously expensive proposition.

Three days, he thought. Something nagged at the back of his mind, suggesting the time until the expedition left was important to him, but he couldn't straighten out his thoughts.

Another headline caught his eye. This was smaller, further down the page:

Moon Hero Sacked by Academy

He usually received very favorable notices in the press. The first paragraph told him this was different. It was short and filled with ugly half-truths and hints that were almost completely wrong. The reporter must have talked to someone at the school, but the story was based on rumors and guesses. It gave the impression that he'd gone temporarily insane on a test flight, nearly wrecked the ship, and been discharged as totally unfit for space. There were implications that for some time he'd been going progressively psychotic and megalomanic.

He read it twice before the suspicion came that Wickman had deliberately told the reporter such a story while pretending to cover up. He couldn't really believe that—Wickman had never lied, so far as he knew—but the suspicion lurked in his mind. Maybe Wickman had said something which the reporter then distorted.

There were no accounts in the other papers at the newsstand, but the late editions were not yet off the press. So far only the local paper had run the story.

He found Wickman on the field, watching the final loading of one of the rocketships. This was an old model, using separate fuel and oxidizer, with a huge bottom stage, a smaller middle stage, and the final stage which carried the passengers and freight into space. It was almost unchanged from the models first used during the building of the Station. Now it towered two hundred feet into the air, its great bulk surrounded by the big gantry cranes.

"Thanks for the paper!" Fred told Wickman bitterly. "I don't know what I'd do without your help."

Wickman turned half smiling, but with no sign of real interest. "Find anything for your clipping file?"

"You should know."

Wickman frowned. "I never got around to reading the paper, so I don't know. What's on your mind, Moon-boy?"

Fred held out the sheet, pointing to the story. Wickman read it through, chuckling once at some line. Then he ripped it up slowly.

"I didn't know it was there. And I didn't have anything to do with it, if that's what you're thinking. Forget it. The Academy will release an official denial and cover-up later, once Olson sees this junk."

Fred grimaced. "Sure. A lot of good that will do, after people read this."

"True. Nothing people like better than seeing a real life hero turn out to be worse than they are. They remember the bad longer than the good. Tough. I guess this will just about ruin all your lecture appearances."

Fred had forgotten the lectures. He'd spent most of his vacation months on a tour of clubs that wanted to hear all about space from the boy who'd made a solo flight to the Moon. It had paid most of his expenses at the Academy, even leaving a healthy surplus which he'd sent to the general fund being raised to help the first colonists on the Moon. He wasn't ashamed of the lectures, though he liked the feeling of attention people gave him almost as much as he liked the fees.

"I wasn't thinking of myself," he said hotly. "My father can read the papers, too, you know."

For a second, Wickman seemed to soften. Then his sneer returned. "You should have thought of that four years ago, Moon-boy," he snapped. "You should have stayed on the Moon, out of his hair."

He moved off to the side, away from Fred and began talking to the co-pilot. A few minutes later, the elevator came down to lift them to the entrance of the ship's final stage. They went through the air lock and into the tiny passenger and control cabin, to strap down in the hammocklike seats and await take-off.

Wickman sat across the narrow aisle, directly behind the co-pilot's seat. A third man sat behind Fred. He was a small, wizened brown man who seemed too old for space, but he must have passed medical inspection to be here. He looked like a Hindu, Fred decided—probably someone from the World Congress. The man sat back now, his eyes closed, and a look of complete joy on his face.

Abruptly, the small man seemed to feel Fred looking at him. He opened startlingly dark eyes and nodded. "Ah, yes. Ramachundra is going into space. To see the stars and the Moon and the cosmos in its true glory. And perhaps even to go as far as the Moon. Yes."

Fred smiled, remembering his own first trip up and how excited he'd been. He'd dreamed of reaching the Moon, too. And however badly he'd done it, he actually had walked on the surface of Earth's satellite. Maybe he should have remained there, as Wickman had suggested.

It hit him then, the idea that had crept into his mind before. The Moon! He'd been denied his chance to be a pilot, and he could only be a nuisance on the Station. There was no place in space for him—except on the Moon. If he could get back there somehow . . .

It wouldn't be easy, though. His only chance was probably with the expedition, if he could persuade them to take him. It was a big *if*. With only three days until the expedition left, the crews and personnel had probably been completed, and he had no skills other than his ability to pilot a ship, now officially denied him.

The pilot put down his radio microphone and called out. "Ten seconds. Five. Three. Two. One."

That was all that remained of the old count-down routine. At zero second, there was a rumbling roar from the rear and the big ship seemed to teeter. It came up from the pad, flame blazing behind it, picked up speed, and streaked toward space.

CHAPTER 4 /

Last Chance

FRED HAD almost forgotten the savage acceleration of the big ships. Here there was no mild feeling of triple weight, but a force that seemed to be bone-crushing. There was a moment of relief when the first stage burned out and dropped off, another at the release of the second. The last thrust, over in seconds, from the third stage's rocket motors was worst of all; then the blast ended and they were suddenly weightless and rising smoothly.

Fred stretched out and unbuckled the straps, holding himself in position with one hand as he turned back to Ramachundra. Greenhorns were usually scared when the first sensation of weightlessness hit them, making them feel they were falling endlessly. Some were sick, and a few even went into convulsions, though the medical examinations eliminated most of those who could not adapt to space.

Ramachundra met his gaze with a beatific smile. "Ah, yes. A glorious thing to be free of gravity, is it not?" He had unbuckled his own straps and now drifted off the seat, holding on with a thumb and finger. "It is as if one were floating astrally outside the body. I have dreamed of this, yes."

Wickman chuckled approvingly. "You're doing great, sir. I thought this was your first trip up."

"True. But since the first tiny satellite crossed over

the skies of my country, I have been here in my thoughts. And I have prepared. Ah yes, I have prepared."

"How?" Fred wanted to know. So far as he knew, there was no good way of preparing for space, except by making trips into it.

The smile deepened. "By a means of my own country, young sir. You may know it as yoga. Oh, no, I see your face shows disbelief. I do not mean the mystic ideas, but the exercises that give one control over the body. Like this, yes."

Without letting go of the seat, the thin, frail-looking man seemed to bend and twist in the air. His legs slid up around his neck until his ankles were clasped together. With a fluid ease, he returned to his former position. The motion had been so smooth it hardly seemed to disturb the position of his torso.

"And there are breathing exercises and many others," Ramachundra said triumphantly. "Until the mind controls all the body. The mind is not afraid of space—that is for the body. You see, perhaps the great technology of the West still has a little to learn from the East. Yes?"

It was a surprising theory on how to adapt to weightlessness. Yet there was a certain amount of sense to the idea. Maybe the Academy had been missing a bet by not having a good course in yoga exercises. Fred kept a doubtful eye on the man for a while, but as the minutes passed he decided Ramachundra really was ready for space.

Anyhow, he had his own problems. One of them was how was he going to explain everything to his father? Colonel Halpern had never understood his son, but Fred knew that his father loved him, somewhere down under the correct military bearing. His expulsion would be a heavy blow to the older man.

The ship glided on effortlessly, losing speed slowly as the minutes passed and they neared the orbit of the Station. Finally, the pilot made the short blast needed to correct their speed and course to that of the Station's orbit. They came to rest a few hundred feet away.

Up here, the big doughnut structure looked huge. More than two hundred feet from rim to rim, it turned slowly around a hub to produce a slight outward force that gave its occupants a sense of gravity. It gleamed brilliantly white in the sunlight, with a little of the immense globe of Earth showing beyond it.

A sausage-shaped space taxi was approaching the ship from the Station and Fred heard it touch against the hull. There was the sound of the airlock being drawn inward, while the taxi's nose exactly filled a silicone ring around the edges to form a seal against loss of air.

Terry Rodriguez was piloting the taxi, Fred saw as he followed the others into the little craft.

"Hi, Freddy," the man greeted him.

Fred tried to grin naturally as he answered, but he knew he'd failed. From the way Terry carefully did not mention anything about his return, he could tell that the news of his washing out was already all over the Station.

"Is Dad in his office?" he asked.

Terry nodded, avoiding his eyes. "Colonel Halpern says to see him as soon as he's finished with Dr. Ramachundra and Major Wickman. In about two hours."

Fred should have known. His father would naturally take care of business before permitting himself to go into the personal troubles of his son. It hurt, but Fred had learned to be proud of his father's sense of duty.

He went into the hub of the Station and took the elevator "down" toward the rim with the others. Weight was about one-third normal there, and he gratefully drew a breath of the thick air into his lungs. It was tainted with smells of oil and chemicals, of cooking and too many people too close together, but it smelled like home to him. All the years on Earth with his grandmother and at the Academy had never meant as much to him as had the time he spent here.

He found the little cabin exactly as he'd left it and transferred the few contents of his bag into the sacks or pouches along the wall. He sat on the hammock that served as a bed, adjusting to his surroundings. Then, amazingly, he found he was bored with it. There was nothing here to see, after all. It was still home, but he was four years older than he'd been when he first lived here. His mind needed more than bare walls and the feeling that he was out in space.

He stood up impatiently and headed for the recreation room where most of the men who were off one of the three shifts and not sleeping spent their time. The rec hall was also unchanged, except for a few worn spots showing in the booths and on the coverings of the stools. He started down the counter toward the coffee machine.

Two men were sitting at the counter, and their voices reached him. One of them dismissed some topic and turned to another. "I hear the Colonel's brat is coming back. Got sacked at school, so he's coming up here again."

"Yeah. He's . . ." The second speaker stopped as he spied Fred out of the corner of his eye. He nudged the other quickly, and swung around on the stool, elaborately casual.

"Hello, Freddy. Heard you were coming back."

Fred forced his feet to go on steadily. "Hello, Dr. Struthers—Mr. Gault. How's the weather below?"

"Today or next year?" Gault asked. It was a standard bad joke on the Station. The two men worked on long-range weather predictions and could usually tell from the cloud patterns what the weather would be next month, but rarely remembered what it was at the moment. They turned back to their coffee, apparently sure Fred hadn't heard them.

He drew a cup of what passed for cocoa here and

wandered back to the rear of the rec hall, where a small port gave a view of space.

The three ships of the expedition were there, small in the distance. Few details showed; they were undoubtedly much like the ones used in the first expedition which he'd seen during their construction. A small dot of light moved near them, indicating a taxi was out there, probably carrying materials for stowage. Most of that work must be done by now, he thought.

A face was reflected in the glass beside his own, and Fred turned to see a stranger. The man was perhaps forty years of age, almost completely bald, and wearing huge glasses that made him seem owl-eyed. His features were sharp and seemed chosen at random giving his face an oddly pleasant ugliness. "Sessions," he introduced himself. "I haven't seen you around before, have I?"

Fred shook his head. "No, sir. I'm Fred Halpern, the Colonel's son." He shook the other's hand, grateful that the man obviously had heard nothing of him. Dr. Sessions was the head of the latest Moon expedition; he had a reputation, built around extensive scientific work, of being a fabulous money-raiser, an excellent leader, and a top-flight geologist as well. Few real scientists seemed capable of heading an expedition; he was the exception.

"Pretty, eh?" Dr. Sessions asked, pointing to the ships. "Not what they should be. I needed twice the money I could get. But they're still pretty. Weren't you the kid who stole a rocket and made a blamed fool jump to the Moon?" He grinned, a dry, amused twisting of his lips. "Yep. I read the papers, too. Was it worth it?"

Fred shook his head. "No, sir. But I'd like to go back there."

This time the man laughed outright.

"You and how many others?" he asked. "People think there's always room for just one more on a trip such as this. Your father's calling me in to twist my arm about some scheme right now. But I'm already carrying two men more than I should. Darts?"

There was a dart board across the hall, and they went over to it. Sessions was not very good, and Fred was worse, although he'd been an expert once. It took time to get the feel of the game under this gravity, despite his knowledge of how the darts should fly.

Finally, Sessions gave up. "Come and have a talk with me in my cabin tonight, if you get a chance, Fred. I read all the junk in the papers, but I never did find why you made that crazy trip out there. I'm curious."

He wandered off, amazingly relaxed for a man who had a million last-minute details to take care of before the expedition left. Fred went on with the darts, having nothing else to do until the loud-speaker summoned him to his father's office.

When he got there, Colonel Halpern was standing beside his desk, wearing the expressionless mask that he always assumed in trying times. He stepped forward to squeeze his son's hand, then dropped back behind the desk.

The room was thick with tension. Colonel Halpern had never been able to deal with Fred as a youngster; even the most trivial pranks upset him. Oddly, as Fred had grown, his father had found it equally hard to accept the fact that the boy was not still a child. Moments of warmth and affection had been rare. Usually, Fred had been in some minor trouble and the older man had been unable to hide his disappointment or to bring the matter out in the open for frank discussion.

"I guess . . ." Fred began.

His father cut him off. "It's done with and we'll forget it. All those years after your mother died . . . Forget it. It's my fault. We'll find something for you to do down on Earth."

"Earth?" Fred asked incredulously.

The Colonel nodded. "The Station's overcrowded. I

can't keep a grown son here. How'd you like to go to MIT? They have the best course in rocket motor design, I understand."

"Dad . . ." Fred began. He couldn't finish.

His father swung back from the desk for a second, staring at a graph on the wall. He cleared his voice and sighed. "Yes, son?"

"I gave most of the lecture money to the Moon Colony Fund," Fred finally said. He couldn't put into words the ideas he wanted to voice. "A good engineering course is expensive."

Colonel Halpern faced him again, straightening resolutely in his chair. "We'll manage. Don't worry about it. We'll find a way. I can still find tuition for my son. Look, we'll talk it over at dinner. Today I'm jammed with business."

At that, Fred thought as he went back toward his cabin, it had gone more easily than most of their recent meetings. Maybe it was because he was older now and had learned not to demand emotions from his father. Or perhaps it was because he'd realized that his father's brusqueness was only a mask hiding the love that he could rarely express.

However, things were worse than Fred had expected. Somehow, he had thought the worst fate for him would be to stay in the Station. He'd never dreamed his dismissal from the Academy would mean his exile to Earth. It meant that his last possible chance was to get on the Moon expedition—and according to Sessions, that was hopeless.

As the day wore on, he could see that his father was right. This was a busy world, with no place for him. He'd been tolerated as a kid, and had even worked at driving the Station's taxi. But now all the jobs were assigned to other men, and he had no skills that were needed here.

He had dinner with his father in the office while they struggled to find something to talk about. They wound up discussing the expedition which was supposed to explore the crust and mineral deposits of the Moon.

"Dr. Sessions tells me he's already overcrowded," Fred said, trying to make conversation.

His father smiled, a little bitterly. "I know. To get extra funds, he has had to take on two extra men from a foundation, so he's overloaded. I was hoping to get a place for Dr. Ramachundra, but that seems hopeless. I don't know—if Ramachundra could get to the Moon and see things as they are . . . Things are going badly at the colony, and I hoped . . ."

He fell silent, clearly bothered with some problem about Ramachundra, and Fred knew enough not to ask about official business. It seemed obvious there was no chance to get any help from his father on the Moon trip. That left only a faint hope which he already knew was futile.

Later, when Fred knocked, Dr. Sessions opened the door of the cabin he was using. He dropped a sheaf of manifold papers onto a shelf which served as his desk and motioned Fred to the hammock. "Go on. I like to stand. Thought you'd forgotten about telling me your story."

"I wasn't sure you really wanted to hear it," Fred answered.

Dr. Sessions laughed. "I'm so busy with useless detail work right now that I'd be glad to have someone read fairy stories to me, Fred. But I've already gotten your story out of Terry Rodriguez. Tell me, did you really think your wild flight made any sense? And how'd you ever manage to land, anyhow?"

Fred wound up telling him more of the story than he'd ever told before, including the horrible time when his ship had toppled over in landing on the Moon and he'd been trapped in it for days until he could be rescued. Somewhere along the line, he found himself talking about Goddard Space Academy.

There were openings in the conversation where he

could have pleaded to go on the expedition, but he found he couldn't ask. If his father wanted to send Ramachundra, it would have been disloyal for Fred to beg for a place. Besides, he quickly realized Dr. Sessions was a man who couldn't be swayed easily, no matter how friendly he seemed.

It was too late the next day. Sessions was out with the expedition, solving the final stowage problems. Fred wandered around, more and more aware of being a nuisance aboard the Station. Maybe an engineering degree in rocket motor design would be the answer. It would still have something to do with space, but he couldn't convince himself that was what he wanted.

He turned in early, trying to read, while the gossip of the Station buzzed through his head. Ramachundra was still in love with space, in spite of his disappointment about the Moon trip. Wickman must have gotten the test pilot's job for the *Cosmic Egg* since Fred saw him leaving in one of the rocketships to Earth, looking pleased with himself. Sessions was planning to load the men of the expedition during the night. And Fred Halpern was going back to Earth. He tossed the book onto a shelf, cut off the light, and tried to sleep.

He was dozing when the emergency gong sounded and a call went out for the Station doctor. Fred got to the rec hall just as a figure, carried on a stretcher, was taken to the infirmary. A minute later, two men, looking shaken and wearing partial spacesuits, came in and headed for the coffee machine.

One of them finally turned to answer the questions being thrown at him. "Some guy from one of the Moon ships. He was crossing from one ship to another, using his rocket pistol for drive. The pistol blew up— defective somehow. Doc says the guy will live, but he's a mess."

There wasn't much more to be learned. Apparently Dr. Sessions had somehow gotten to the wounded men and made an almost impossible success of patching up his spacesuit before he died from lack of air. It was an ugly accident.

For a second, Fred hesitated, looking toward his father's office. Then he sighed and gave up the idea. Maybe this meant that another man could be taken on the expedition. But if so, that man would be Ramachundra. He knew his father well enough to be sure of that.

He waited until the news came that the injured man was going to live, and then left the rec hall, along with most of the crowd. He was less sleepy than before, however. This time he managed to make a start in the book.

The speaker in the hallway hooted for attention and began issuing a call. "Fred Halpern. Calling Fred Halpern. You're wanted in the Colonel's office, immediately. Report to the Colonel's office immediately."

CHAPTER 5 /

Unwelcome Guest

HE WAS running down the hallway before the speaker stopped its clamor, trying to tell himself it meant nothing at all. It might only be that the wounded man needed blood that matched his blood type. He couldn't remember what that was, but they had it on file in the Station. But he didn't believe anything like that. It had to be something else, if the summons was to his father's office.

There were two men in the office when he entered—his father and Dr. Sessions. Colonel Halpern looked weary, as if he'd skipped sleep again, but the mask was off now. Under the official expression of command was something else.

Sessions turned toward Fred, and there was nothing of his normal ease about him. "Read that," he suggested.

It was a typed transcript of a wireless message. The Station's position must be too far from the message station on Earth for voice signals. It was addressed to Dr. Sessions. "Regret inform you Halpern considered unfit for space. Technical skill as pilot excellent. Personal qualities unreliable." It was signed by Commandant Olson.

"I told you all that, Dr. Sessions," Fred protested.

"I know you did. That's why I called Olson about you. I had to know whether you were a skilled pilot or not. This simply confirms your own story." Sessions stared at the boy, analyzing him. "You heard about the accident? Of course, of course. Well, the man was one of my co-pilots. There isn't another pilot here, and Earth informs me no ship can be fitted and fueled for at least twelve hours. That's too late—I'm cutting it fine enough as it is, without leaving when the Moon isn't in its best position. So I'm desperate."

He paused for a second, and Colonel Halpern broke in. "Freddy, are you up to a Moon landing if something should happen to the pilot?"

"Of course I am, Dad." There was no question about that in his mind. He'd managed a fair landing with almost no training and three years at the Academy had fitted him for almost any job in space. "But I don't have a license, and Dr. Sessions can't leave without licensed pilot and co-pilot."

"I'll issue a temporary license, like those we use for all the taxi pilots," the Colonel told him.

Dr. Sessions nodded. "Fine. Only I want one thing understood, Fred. You're still an unknown quantity to me, and I'm only taking you out of necessity. I'll expect absolute obedience. In space or on the Moon, I can have a man executed for mutiny if he fails to obey. And I warn you, if you can't take discipline after what I'm saying now, I'll consider you a mutineer sooner than I would anyone else. Under those conditions, do you want to sign on as co-pilot?"

"When do we leave, sir?" Fred asked.

Colonel Halpern sighed softly, and one of his rare smiles appeared. "Good man!" he exclaimed. It was the first time he'd ever called Fred a man.

Sessions still didn't look happy about the arrangement, but he smiled faintly. "Better get to the ship as soon as you can. You'll be on the *Kepler*. We leave in three hours."

This was long before the time given out publicly, but that wasn't surprising. Fred had guessed it already from the Moon's position, and had realized that the later time was given out to prevent the passengers becoming nervous in the last hour before take-off.

Sessions turned and left. Colonel Halpern came around the desk, looking awkward and pleased. He held out his hand. "I won't have a chance to see you off, Fred, so I'll wish you good luck now. You're on your own. Make the most of it."

"I'll try, Dad," Fred promised him. He gripped his father's hand, then walked quickly to the door. He hesitated with the door half open. Then he blurted out in a rush, "I'll miss you, Dad."

Halpern looked up quickly, the smile spreading on his face. "Me too," he told Fred. "God bless you, boy."

Outside the door, Fred stopped at the first corner, bracing himself against the wall until the trembling in his legs stopped. He'd given up all hope, and then this had happened. It was too much to believe at once, and the physical reaction left him momentarily weak. Then it passed, and he headed for his cabin to pack. He had to get to the *Kepler* in time for briefing.

The pilot of the *Kepler* turned out to be Poorhouse, a veteran of other Moon expeditions. Fred knew him slightly, and it was plain that Poorhouse remembered the boy he had seen first four years before. He didn't look happy when he discovered the identity of his copilot.

"You probably won't have a thing to do," he explained. "But if you do, you'll have to be ready for it. Better memorize all this."

There were pages of charts, instructions and figures. The course was exactly what Fred had known it must be, and he went through the charts only to satisfy Poorhouse. His eyes were mostly busy studying the two other ships visible through the control port. Since the ships would never operate in an atmosphere, there was no streamlining. They were built of uncovered girders that supported the motors and storage tanks for freight.

The passenger compartment was another rounded tank at the front, and the tanks of fuel and oxidizer were huge plastic balloons, fastened on the outside where they could be scuttled when empty. Fred estimated the amount of fuel, then turned back to the manifest showing the amount of supplies they were carrying. It hardly seemed that they could carry it all.

Abruptly, he remembered that the colony on the Moon finally had managed to get the making of fuel and liquid oxygen into production. The materials were common enough, available in the rocks, and the un-shielded sunlight gave them enough power for the chemical operations. Oxygen was something they had to bake and electrolyze out of gypsum for their air, any-how.

The ships could carry much more cargo on this expe-dition, since they were not forced to take along fuel for the return trip. Fuel would be supplied by the colonists in exchange for supplies and equipment left after the expedition was over. Such things were desperately needed by the colony.

There was a stirring behind him and he looked back to see Poorhouse checking on the seat belts of the eight men and women passengers on the *Kepler*. In a few minutes, the pilot came forward and took his seat, con-ferring by radio with the pilots of the other ships.

When take-off came, there was nothing for Fred to do. He watched Poorhouse maneuver the controls. The man had been piloting for years, yet there was some-thing sloppy about his work. He'd never been one of the best pilots, and he hadn't improved. Yet he seemed con-fident enough.

The acceleration was fairly low, since the ships were not designed for the heavy drive needed in the ships that left from Earth. They began pulling away from the Station and spiraling out toward the orbit of the Moon, heading for where the Moon would be five days from now. The blast went on at this low acceleration far longer than would have been necessary for the rise from Earth. Two-thirds of their speed came from the rotational motion they already had around Earth in the Station orbit.

Finally the blast was cut. Poorhouse had drifted away from the others. Fred began feeding information into the calculator at random, pretending to study the instruments carefully. He was putting in the final figures from the correction his mind had automatically supplied when the radio speaker buzzed.

"Trim your course, Mr. Poorhouse," the voice of Lee Yeng ordered; he was the chief pilot, aboard Dr. Sessions' *Copernicus*.

Fred passed over the final figures, tearing off the tape to make it seem that they were the sum of his other figures. Poorhouse grunted in surprise, looked doubtful, and then nodded.

"I guess the new Academy education must be good for something," he said. "Thanks. But get ready to run a new set if you're off a little."

He managed the controls somewhat better this time, using only one small blast to correct a tiny error that had crept into his piloting. He waited until the speaker acknowledged that the maneuver was correct. "Pretty good, Halpern. You had it figured dead right. Glad to have you aboard."

It was a formal statement that should have been made when Fred first entered the ship, but still gratifying. "Thank you, Mr. Poorhouse. Glad to be aboard. Shall I go out and remove the empty tanks?"

Poorhouse considered it, and nodded. It was a job Fred had read about in accounts of previous expeditions. He climbed into his spacesuit, tested his oxygen supply, and dropped down toward the air lock. As he passed through it, he could see Earth, growing smaller. The ship was moving nearly seven miles a second. Since his speed and that of the ship were exactly the same, it felt as if he were standing on a motionless hull. The maze of girders and cables gave him enough handholds as he worked his way around, unlatching the manual releases on the emptied fuel tanks. The full ones would remain, since their contents would be used in landing. There was a small spring in each release that gave a slight outward push to the tanks and sent them drifting off slowly, beyond the path of the ship. It was easy work to anyone used to moving about in space, and completely safe; if he should drift away, there was always the tiny rocket pistol to use for getting back.

That was the last interesting thing for three days. The ships drifted outward toward the Moon, losing speed gradually as Earth's gravity pulled at them. The men on board ate and slept and talked.

Most of it was technical talk about the geology—or the selenology—of the Moon, and what they might learn. Fred couldn't follow it. Poorhouse was reading from a small microfilm set of books; they were all mystery stories, and Fred had never learned to like such fiction, even if there had been a spare reader. Space looked unchanging; the emptiness was jet black, and the stars tiny bright points, appearing farther away than when seen from Earth's atmosphere.

The time seemed endless until they reached the position where the Moon's pull was stronger than that of Earth. Now they began picking up speed again, while the pilots used gyroscopes to turn the ships slowly, pointing the rockets toward the Moon instead of toward Earth.

It was near the end of the fourth day that Fred discovered trouble. He had been running the landing figures through the computer for want of anything better to do. He already knew the results, of course, and the figures on the tape were a long way off.

At his signal, Poorhouse bent over and they conferred in low voices, not wanting to disturb the passengers. Poorhouse checked the computer. He was slow and uncertain about it, but his results were even further off.

"Busted," he agreed. He reached for the microphone.

Fred stared at the computer doubtfully. "I guess it doesn't matter," he decided. "We know the figures."

"We've still got to correct for any errors in maneuvers," Poorhouse told him. "A ship without a computer might as well be blind."

"I can give you the correction figures out of my head," Fred said. "I've done it before in school and . . ."

"School orbits!" Poorhouse grunted. "I suppose you'd be willing to trust your life to seat-of-the-pants piloting, would you? Nonsense."

He began reporting the trouble over the radio. Fifteen minutes later there was a thump on the air lock and Fred let in a slim girl in a spacesuit. She shucked it quickly and began pulling tiny instruments out of a number of zippered pockets in her shorts.

"Can you fix it?" Poorhouse asked, as she bent over the computer.

She snorted. "I can fix the monster we're using for running our sub-surface Moon graphs," she told him. "This thing is easy."

Fred scowled. Women might be as good as men in space, or even better, as some books claimed. But he didn't trust a girl with machinery—particularly one who considered a repair job too simple. He'd had his personal radio ruined by a repairwoman who scoffed at it as an easy job. But at least he understood why they had someone to repair the machine; an expedition using electronic gadgets in the exploring work would need an expert.

"There—two transistors burned out. Simple." She wired the tiny things in place with a smoothness that almost convinced Fred and put the cover back.

Poorhouse laughed. "Better check the transistors in

Fred's head, too. We may need them. Oh. Mona Williams, this is Fred Halpern."

She flashed a grin at Fred, but shook her head at the suggestion until Poorhouse told her of Fred's plan to figure the corrections in his head. Then she began laughing—a laughter in which the other passengers joined quickly, more out of boredom than because they could understand.

Okay, Fred thought. Next time, maybe he'd keep his mouth shut. He went back to his seat, flushing angrily until Mona had gone. But that wasn't the end of the affair. Ten minutes later, the speaker buzzed. "Mr. Halpern." The voice was Dr. Sessions'.

"Here, sir."

"Mr. Halpern, I'm told you suggested landing by mental figuring without using your computer. I want an explanation."

Fred sighed, realizing there was no sense in telling the whole story. He'd skimmed over that part of his trouble at the Academy, so apparently Sessions hadn't paid any attention to it. "I didn't know the computer could be repaired. I'm good with orbits, and I thought I should offer."

Sessions seemed uncertain. Finally he grunted. "Okay. In that case, your offer is appreciated. But you'll do your piloting by computer."

Poorhouse came back to the control seat, tapping his head and making little orbits in the air with one finger. It was a fine joke to him. Fred had a suspicion that the pilot's main trouble was his inability to plot accurate corrections on the computer; thus it wasn't hard to see why he couldn't conceive of anyone with a gift for sensing the complicated vector mathematics involved.

The Moon was growing bigger and the ships rushing toward the rendezvous when the order came to start decelerating for the landing. At a signal from Lee Yeng, Poorhouse began applying power to slow their fall toward the ugly, pockmarked surface still hundreds of miles away.

"You're off course, Mr. Poorhouse," Lee's voice rapped out.

Poorhouse glanced toward Fred, who was already making the computation. It was slower using the computer than figuring it out in his head, but he was following orders. He could do it faster than Poorhouse.

Then he caught his breath as the answer came out. One half of it was right, but the other half was complete nonsense. Mona had been too sure. She must have fixed the machine, but she hadn't checked thoroughly enough to see that something else was wrong—wrong enough to burn out the new transistors, as it had burned out the old ones. Poorhouse was waiting impatiently—and now there was no other solution.

Fred rattled off the figures from his head, pretending he was reading them from the tape. Poorhouse nodded, and began setting up the controls. The blast altered slightly, and the *Kepler* drifted over toward the path of its fellow ships. Again, Fred made motions over the computer, punching it at random, and pretending to read the answer. The new setting brought them into a smooth descent beside the two other ships.

"You're a first-class computer operator, even if you do have illusions," Poorhouse said in satisfaction. "We make a good team, at that."

He seemed more confident as he took the later figures Fred supplied. He was not a poor pilot; he was just uncertain of his plotting and that ruined his control. Now his piloting firmed up, as he began to trust the course coördinates Fred gave him. They came rushing down toward the landing area near Emmett Base, now marked out with small radio beacons that made control possible even when the surface was invisible in the glare of the rocket blasts. Fred never felt the impact as the ship touched down finally and cut off the blast automatically. Only the silence told him they had landed.

Poorhouse was obviously delighted with the landing. He slapped Fred across the shoulders as he got up with the log to report to Sessions and then to the Base. "You've been here before, Fred. Bring out the others and have them walk around to get the feel of it while I report in."

Fred took over. It wasn't as difficult as it would have been without the experience the expedition members already had at the Station. This made it easier to adjust to the idea that gravity didn't always pull down with the same force as on Earth, although here it was only one-sixth normal. It took an hour before he could trust his group to begin unloading the first bulky cases from the ship. By that time Poorhouse was back. The pilot touched helmets with him.

"Governor Gantry wants to see you, Fred," he said. His voice was muffled by the helmet, but the words were understandable. "You'll see a big marker at the base of the cliff there. I'll take over here."

Fred checked the oxygen in his tank and headed across the glaring, cracked rocky plateau where they'd landed, enjoying the sensation of being on the Moon. And apparently this was one place where he was remembered without dislike. Gantry had never paid much attention to him before, but it would be good to see the governor of the colony. He found a crude set of steps, leading downward, hammered out of the cliff. At the bottom, the only light was reflected from the sunlight striking the upper cliff. He slipped the dark visor up inside his helmet until he could make out the Administration sign. It led to an air lock at one end of a small Quonset-type hut. Inside, the light was brighter, and he had to blink before he could make out the huge figure of Gantry.

Gantry was alone in the hut, and made no effort to get up to greet Fred.

"So the bad penny turns up again." The voice was low, but the words were clear enough. "And from what

I hear, you're the same Freddy Halpern you were four years ago."

Fred stared at him in shocked amazement. Here, where he'd been certain of a reasonable welcome if only because of the money from his lectures which he'd sent the colony, he seemed to be the Moon's number one unwanted guest.

CHAPTER 6/

Lunar Colony

ABRUPTLY, the stiffness seemed to run out of Gantry. His big figure slumped over the stone slab that served as a desk and his hands went up wearily to shove the iron-gray hair back on his head.

"Sorry," he said. "That wasn't the way I meant to say it. Sit down a minute and let me get my thoughts straight."

Before Fred could move to the seat indicated, the air lock hissed and another man came through it. The spacesuit was worn and patched, and the plastic helmet was clouded with scratches. There was something familiar about the figure inside it. Fred gasped as the helmet came off.

"Mr. Jonas!"

"Freddy!" Jonas gave an answering whoop and trotted forward, his arms outstretched. "Freddy, it's great to see you again! Man, how you've grown. And filled out. You're a sight for sore eyes."

Fred studied the man before him, conscious that more changes had taken place in four years than his own growing up. Jonas had always seemed like the perfect picture of a successful businessman; he'd been one of the top men in industry, yet he'd given up all that to organize the colony here. He was thinner, with deep folds of skin where fat had been once, and his hair was snow-white. Only his eyes were the same, twinkling with a keen awareness of every detail.

He looked around quickly, seeming to take in the whole situation. "What's going on here?"

"Governor Gantry is telling me I'm not welcome on the Moon," Fred answered.

Jonas snorted in disbelief. "Nonsense. We know of what you've tried to do to help us. We haven't forgotten who our friends are, Fred."

"I guess it came out that way," Gantry said. "Look, Fred, I like you. I always did. But I can't afford to trust you. You played the hero once and almost wrecked things for us. Maybe you've changed, but showing off to Poorhouse on the flight here, trying to be the great man who doesn't need a computer, reminds me of the same kid I knew. And that kid was a fool. Well, we can't afford fools. The smallest slip here can kill a man, and maybe kill a lot of others with him. So cut out the idea of pulling some great stunt and stick to doing what you have to do reliably. That's all I meant to say in the first place."

Put that way, it was better, Fred realized, but the meaning wasn't much different. He still wasn't wanted until he could prove himself. How could a man prove himself unless he did try to do something important enough to be noticed? He said doubtfully, "I'll try."

"Good." Gantry ended that part of the discussion. "Stick around and we'll try to show you the colony. Jonas, did you see the manifest of shipment?"

"Bad?" the other asked.

It was worse than just bad, from what Fred could gather. The sponsors of the expedition had made arrangements for the colony to provide fuel for the return and were supposed to pay for it with certain materials and tools desperately needed here. When the funds began to vanish too quickly, the sponsors were unable to live up to their bargain. At least half of what was most needed had not been brought along.

"Clever men," Jonas commented bitterly. "They know perfectly well we can't refuse the fuel for the return, no matter what happens. So they save money by cutting our throats. Was Dr. Sessions part of this?"

"He knew about it," Gantry answered. "But what could he do? He had to take what they gave him."

Fred began to get some idea of the troubles here. He'd known of them before, but they had been distant problems; now, faced with the worry and desperation of the two men, he sensed the urgency of it all.

The colony at Emmett Base had to be self-sustaining in the long run. Freighting material from Earth was so tremendously expensive that nothing the colony could produce would make it profitable. The only solution was to make everything needed on the Moon, which required more tools and power than they had. The two previous expeditions had helped by leaving behind their surplus supplies. Money from films and books, and contributions like those from Fred's lectures, had helped, but there had never been enough. With the United States going through an economy drive, there was no hope of American aid, either.

They had licked part of the problem when they found a way to make fuel. Until it was worn beyond repair, they'd been able to freight supplies from the Station in one of the ships left behind on the second expedition. The present expedition was their last hope, and a feeble one at best. Time was running out. They were short of everything. Even with the supplies the expedition should have brought, the colony couldn't be sure of existing for more than another six months.

"If we found uranium, so we could build a nuclear power reactor, we might make out," Jonas summed it up to Fred. "Or if we could get one of those new monopropellant ships. Peevy, our chemical engineer, says we can synthesize the monopropellant. In fact, with enough power and basic tools we could make anything. All the basic elements are here. Maybe, if Halpern could have found some way for Dr. Ramachundra to get here . . ."

"He couldn't and there's no proof Ramachundra would do that much good. So we'll have to go it alone," Gantry stated flatly.

Jonas took Fred around the little base. There wasn't much to see, but it represented four years of tremendous work. Except for the Administration hut, all the "buildings" were hollowed out of the soft rock of the cliffs. Sprayed plastic made the rooms airtight, and a central tunnel providing air and communication connected all dwellings. At regular intervals, doors in the tunnel could be slammed to cut off any section developing a leak. A whole family might live in a single room no more than eight feet by ten feet. Even the furniture was carved out of the rock whenever possible, and beds were niches cut into the walls.

On the flat plateau across the crevasse from the landing field, the solar power station had been built. This was an arrangement of mirrors that directed the sunlight onto a big tank that served as a boiler to provide steam to drive a turbine and generator.

"What do you do during the fourteen days of darkness?" Fred asked.

"Run off stored power. During two weeks of light, we use a lot of the power to break water down into hydrogen and oxygen. We've got a couple of big natural caverns back that way to serve as tanks. Then, when it's dark, we run the steam generator by burning the hydrogen and oxygen back to water. It isn't efficient, but it's the best we can do."

The problem seemed to be mostly a matter of accumulating reserve energy until they could build some proper source of power. They had found a vein of copper and a mine where low-grade iron ore could be worked. There were plenty of aluminum compounds. But getting the metal out of the ores required tremendous power, as did the casting and forging of parts.

Once they could get over what Jonas called the "hump," where new developments yielded more than the cost in effort, they would be all right. Until then, the drain on their energy plant was greater than the return, meaning the deficit had to be made up in shipments from Earth.

They came to a larger room which was the central kitchen. Here a group of tiny, very hot hydrogen flames were serving as stoves, and the women of the colony were preparing a meal to be eaten in the community dining room. The food seemed to be entirely vegetables. It looked and tasted good, but it must grow monotonous, and was hardly an ideal diet.

Jonas pointed out the big gardens. These were set on the floor of the shallowest part of the crevasse, where sunlight could reach them easily, though artificial lights had to be used for long periods. The individual sections were roofed over with transparent plastic, and plants of all kinds were growing in beds of crushed rock and chemically fertilized soil. It was the source of most of the food and fresh air for the colony. Keeping a suitable temperature range during the hot day and freezing night was a problem.

"Why do you stick it out?" Fred asked.

But the question was needless. Fred couldn't put it into words, but he'd known years before that he must leave Earth and get into space. There was a drive inside him to push back the frontier, to escape from the narrow limits of a single world. Like the people around him now, he felt that he belonged here—and that, in times to come, he'd probably belong even farther out, on other planets, perhaps some day around other stars. The only problem was to find some means by which he could join and remain in a group moving back the last frontiers.

During the next couple of "days"—shifts were adjusted to Earth time—Fred found work could be just as hard here as anywhere else. The low gravity made lifting and carrying easier, but destroyed all the habits of muscular coördination. Even work in the Station hadn't been quite the same.

They were unloading the ships and transferring the supplies to a base down in the crevasse. A dome of thin plastic had been set up there under a ledge to form a depot. Sessions insisted that all the supplies and equipment must be carefully inspected. A failure out on the Moon could mean death, and no precautions against defective equipment were too great. To Fred's surprise, he discovered that some of the equipment needed going over; apparently no one on Earth could imagine the closeness of danger existing here, and some of the work had been careless. One of the tractor motors took a full day of adjustment before it was dependable. It ran on the breakdown of hydrogen peroxide, like the fuel pumps on the ships; water and heat were the results of this action and they combined to form steam. Since the colony could produce the peroxide, it was the most practical fuel for motors on the airless moon.

Fred found time for further inspection of the colony; he was amazed at the number of products they had been able to turn out from available supplies such as stone. They hoarded their metals for use where nothing else would do. Glass and plastics were scarce; these materials had to be shipped from Earth, since making them required special tools and too much power. With all their inventiveness, the colonists were poorer in possessions than the most impoverished settlers in the early days of America.

Yet the people were eager to go on. They never seemed bored or sorry they were here. If they weren't happy, it was only because they knew the end of the colony was only months away.

Apparently Jonas and Gantry had counted too much on the interest of Earth to get the colony started. Earth wasn't much interested. Once the two great blocs of nations—the Combine in the East and the Alliance in the

West—had agreed that space was international, the drive to beat each other stopped. The people seemed content that men had already conquered space, and would not stand for the taxation that further exploration required. The Station was obviously valuable for weather predictions, and money for that could be found; but so far there were no benefits to be gained from the Moon. So why waste the taxpayers' money?

The name of Ramachundra came up frequently. Fred asked for more details, but could learn little. All that was known was that the little man had been appointed by the World Congress to investigate the colony in any way he chose. It could mean nothing at all, though the World Congress had grown much stronger in the last few years as the minor nations began to make full use of it.

Fred became somewhat sensitive about the whole business, since it was clear the colonists resented his coming, as if it had prevented Ramachundra's. The Hindu couldn't have piloted the ship, but that fact did not stop the feeling he should have come instead of Fred.

They also bitterly resented the *Cosmic Egg*. Word came over the radio that the *Egg* had been successful on its first test flight to the Station. It had been piloted by Wickman, Fred discovered, with a feeling of resentment. To the Moon, the *Egg* would have meant the possibility of surviving and transporting needed supplies from Earth. The colonists couldn't understand why it was developed for use from Earth to the Station. It seemed as if Earth had deliberately created the answer to the colonists' needs and then had selfishly kept it away from the Moon.

Nevertheless, they went on fighting. The mines, some distance from the Base, were being worked as fully as possible. They were also going ahead with plans for a new location for the colony.

Jonas showed Fred the plans one day after dinner.

Fred had brought his rations with him, to add to the common meal; he was deeply touched by how much a little variety added to their fare meant to these people. After dinner, Jonas took him into the Administration hut to see the sketches.

They had found a group of connected caverns not far from the mines. What caused these caverns in a world without air and water was still a mystery, but the usual explanation was that ancient gas bubbles had been trapped under the cooling crust. In any event, once the caverns could be connected and sealed against air loss, they would provide shelter and a great deal more space than the colony now had. It might be possible to establish a city of several thousand in such a place, once the tremendous work of preparing them and partitioning them was finished.

Jonas put the plans away regretfully. "That's for the future, though. If there is a future. What we need is something that will attract the interest of Earth enough to bring help or get a bunch of expeditions going. Only a near miracle will save us. Maybe finding some kind of life here would do it."

"I thought the scientists of all the expeditions reported no sign of life," Fred commented.

"They did. But I'm not sure they're right. Some of our people claim they've seen signs to indicate something was growing here—some kind of plant." Jonas' eyes got the hungry look Fred was learning to expect from the colonists. "That would bring an interest, all right. If there's any type of life at all here, things would hum long enough to get us set up."

There were a lot of *ifs,* and none of them looked like very hopeful ones.

Dr. Sessions was waiting for Fred when he came back. The expedition leader sat in the control room of the *Kepler,* where Fred still slept, and his face was stern.

"Your computer doesn't work," he announced. "I

tried to solve a simple problem on it, and got gibberish. Did you know that?"

Fred nodded reluctantly, and the scientist frowned more deeply. "All right, then. Did you disable it, Fred?"

"No, sir. I think there's a short somewhere in the power supply."

"Why didn't you report it?"

Fred shook his head. He'd been trying to find an excuse that wouldn't reveal the fact he'd plotted the landing without using it. "There was no time. I only found the trouble again when we were landing. And Mona Williams hasn't had time to work on it since."

"All right." Sessions seemed to drop the problem from his mind. "I hope you're telling the truth. If you are, I owe you a lot. If not, you're a fool. It won't matter now, anyhow. The expedition pulls out tomorrow. Maybe you can get the computer fixed before we return."

Surprise hit Fred at that. "But—but I thought we'd all go."

"No—not the pilots," Dr. Sessions said. "Pilots are very special people. They aren't supposed to do dirty work. They're the glamour boys of space. They fixed the rules three years ago so they don't even help loading cargo. Oh, I meant to thank you for your help there, Fred." He nodded his indebtedness. "But all you have to do is stay here and watch the ships."

Fred frowned, remembering that the other pilots hadn't worked, now that he thought of it. It seemed strange to him, particularly when Sessions was short-handed. The leader had stressed that he wanted to time the return for fourteen weeks after the landing, but admitted it might take eighteen weeks; the trip could only be made at four-week intervals because of the position of the Moon.

Four weeks could make a good deal of difference in the amount of supplies thirty people would consume—

that could mean a lot to the colonists, since any remaining goods would be left for them.

"I'd like to come, sir," he suggested. "That is, if you can find any work I can do. I'm not trained for much except piloting."

"You could probably operate a tractor. You have good eyes and quick reflexes. I suppose you had a course in fuel pump motor maintenance at the Academy, so you should be a better tractor mechanic than any of the men I have. The co-pilot you replaced had volunteered for the job, and I was counting on him. I wish I could trust you." Sessions considered it. His eyes clouded for a second as he glanced at the computer. Then he shrugged.

Fred could think of nothing to prove his trustworthiness. He waited silently as the scientist studied him.

"All right, Fred," Dr. Sessions said finally. "I've been trying to persuade Gantry to assign a driver from the colony, but none can be spared. If you can take the discipline out there, I can use you. Get some sleep and be ready in the morning. It's going to be tough, and you'd better start out rested."

He left, and Fred tried to follow his advice. But his mind was full of doubts. There had been so much said about his glory-hogging that he couldn't be sure of himself any longer. Yet he honestly felt that his going would help the colony. He wasn't looking for glory any more than he had been when necessity forced him to plot the landing without the computer.

He wondered how difficult it would be to take the discipline Dr. Sessions kept emphasizing. Just how tough was it out there on the surface of the Moon, cut off from both ships and colony?

CHAPTER 7 /

World of Death

IN SPITE OF Dr. Sessions' financial troubles, the expedition was far better equipped than the previous ones for traveling across the Moon. Already much had been learned by experience.

There were three tractors, looking like early model military tanks with certain modifications. These had larger viewing ports at the front and sides, tracks made of a silicone rubber of tremendous strength, and a thin, reflective sheet of metal raised over each to shield it from the heat of the sun during the lunar day.

Each tractor would haul one large and one small trailer. The small ones were for equipment and supplies, and resembled low boxes riding on four wheels. One of the larger trailers carried most of the scientific instruments and formed an office and laboratory, while the other two were compact quarters for the men and for the women of the expedition. These were not unlike automobile trailers, except that they were lower, with more wheels. They had to be airtight and equipped with air locks, of course, and they also carried screens to shield them from the sun.

Fred found Dr. Sessions waiting inside his tractor when he came down after breakfast. He managed to smile at the sight. There was plenty of room for three or four people in the tractor, but Sessions would normally have ridden in the more comfortable laboratory. His presence could only mean he wasn't certain of his new tractor driver.

Sessions smiled back, as if acknowledging the fact, but he said nothing about it. Instead he glanced at his watch. "We'll get rolling in about ten minutes. I hear you were out getting used to the machine."

"I thought I'd better, sir," Fred said. He'd spent an hour in practice with the control levers—one for each track—which steered the tractor. "It isn't very difficult."

"No, I suppose not, if you're mechanically inclined. Familiar with the general course?"

Fred nodded. He'd studied the maps. The other expeditions had kept to a limited distance from Emmett Base; this one was to go on into new territory. For the first day, they'd be following trails already marked. After that, they would have to depend on photographs in picking the trail. On the Moon, such photographs weren't as helpful as they might be, since the shadows were too black and the highlights too white for fine details to show. Their course westward would be mostly a matter of trial and error.

"You'll lead off," Sessions said. "You're the youngest driver and you probably have the best reflexes in case of trouble. Also, I'd rather lose the lab than one of the trailers with people in it. Might as well get started."

Fred fed power into the motor carefully. It was under the floor, and a faint hissing was transmitted from it. He took a deep breath and reached for the levers. The tractor began moving, with slight jerks as the trailers were brought into motion. They picked up speed slowly until they were traveling at nearly ten miles an hour. In the mirror, Fred could see the other two tractors following.

Sessions sat back and relaxed, though his eyes were still busy. However, the convoy was traveling over a flat crater bed, where there wasn't much to worry about.

"I suppose you got most of your idea of what we're

after from the papers?" he asked Fred casually. "Of course. You weren't briefed, since we didn't expect you to go out with us. Well, it doesn't much matter, since we've got plenty of time for briefing later."

"I'm a little curious," Fred said. He suspected the older man was planning to do most of the briefing right then, and he welcomed it.

Most of it was quite technical, and he had only a dim knowledge of geology. Sessions began with what the other expeditions had found. They'd charted a number of craters and pretty well established that some of the craters were caused by meteorites; they'd even found a meteorite in the bottom of one very small crater. There were evidences of lava flow in other places, indicating that the Moon once must have had a hotter core, and there was still some activity going on. Gas was seeping up from fumaroles. The expeditions had determined the normal level of radiation on the Moon and found it quite low. They'd looked unsuccessfully for life. The old idea that there might be a layer of matter related to life just under the surface hadn't proved true, though a few dead spores were found which might have drifted all the way from Earth. They'd also found that the great rays seemed to be splashed across the surface as if light material had been thrown up volcanically, but they had no idea of the real cause of these formations.

"It doesn't sound as if they'd accomplished much," Fred observed.

"The scientific work doesn't sound like much," Sessions agreed. "But you'd be surprised how the general picture of Earth and the Moon is changing because now we have a few exact measurements. Earth was also studied through a telescope, you know. You must have heard of that."

Fred had heard—probably there was no one who hadn't learned of the great iron ore deposits in Africa located through hints in photographs taken from the Moon.

The present expedition was of a different kind. Instead of trying to learn a little about everything, it was expected to make an intensive study of the Moon's crust, which seemed to hold the key to most of the remaining puzzles. One area toward which they were heading seemed to have the greatest promise for discovery. They hoped to locate deposits of ore that might be useful to colonists here, and they would keep a careful watch for evidence of uranium. The major research tools would be the sensitive instruments that could measure ground shocks from tiny explosions, analyzing the way they spread through the surface and bounced back from deeper layers.

They came to a stop for lunch. Better time could have been made by using relief drivers, but Sessions believed that it paid in the long run to stick to an Earth-type day and night schedule. After traveling any distance, he felt it wise to check machines and give the men real rest that couldn't be had in the pitching motion over the surface. When lunch was over, he motioned Fred back into the tractor, then headed for the headquarters laboratory himself. Although he could keep in touch by radio, Fred felt it was a sign of confidence, and it made him feel better.

They were coming into unmarked territory when they halted for dinner, inspection and sleep. There was a range of low mountains ahead through which they had to break a trail, and that would be rough going. He and the other drivers spent half an hour with Sessions, going over the best possible route. Finally Fred snapped his helmet down, checked his oxygen tank automatically, and picked up a metal-foil umbrella. In the glaring heat from the sun, the umbrella was a necessity. There was a hummock of rock ahead; it should be possible to get a better view of the jagged mountains from that. Sessions came along.

The trail they had picked still looked best, however, and they headed back toward the trailers, bending their course around a couple of jagged boulders. As they moved back, Fred spotted another figure coming toward them, trotting along at a rate deceptively easy in the light gravity and brushing against one of the rocks.

Fred let out a yell, flipping on his radio transmitter. The approaching figure seemed not to notice; perhaps its receiver wasn't on. With another yell, Fred dived for the figure, catching it around the waist and yanking it back from the rocks. Then his eyes widened as he saw the oxygen gauge. He lifted the spacesuited body over his head and began running toward the nearest trailer; in spite of the kicking going on, it wasn't too hard to handle such a weight for a few hundred feet in the low gravity.

Sessions was already ahead, working the air lock. They piled through it quickly, and Fred unlocked the helmet and tossed it back to show the angry face and coppery hair of Mona Williams.

She started to say something, but Sessions cut her off. "Silence!" His voice was sharp enough to quiet her anger and to bring the rest of the company up from the social discussion that had been going on. "You probably just had your life saved, young lady. All right, Fred. You know space conditions. You tell her."

Fred was panting a little, but he found his voice almost as stern as Sessions. "There were a lot of things. First, no umbrella . . ."

"For that little distance?" she cut in.

"For any distance. By the time you feel the heat through your helmet, it's too late. These new suits are easier to wear, but they don't have the insulating and cooling capacity of the older model space suits. Second, you were scraping your suit against the rocks. Those rocky outcroppings have sharp points, and it doesn't take much to put a hole in a suit. And third, you hadn't checked the meters for your radio batteries—which were dead—or your oxygen tank, which was empty."

"And finally," Sessions said grimly, "I gave orders

nobody was to go outside alone under any conditions. It isn't the first time you've been impatient with details and orders, Dr. Williams. Maybe you'll have time to think it over during the next week, since you'll do all the cleaning up after meals. And the next time, I won't be so easy on anyone."

There were mutters of protest, and he swung to face the group.

"You've heard about it, now you'd all better realize it—you're out in the middle of a world of sudden, sometimes horrible death. Anyone of the seemingly little things Mr. Halpern mentioned could kill a man— and would, if he were alone. There are temperature extremes, lack of air, and unknown terrain, all threatening you. Beside this, life at the South Pole or in the worst jungles is simple. The only way we can live is to use our heads. You'd better learn that. Anyone who hasn't been in space before has to take any advice either Mr. Halpern or I give you. Otherwise, the first time you get careless or forget, we may have to bury you."

The going was tougher the next day, as they began moving into mountainous country. Here the photographs of the area taken from above were less reliable than elsewhere. Jagged rocks were everywhere. The tractors could climb over fairly rough obstacles, and the multiple wheels of the trailers were almost as effective. But nothing could scale a cliff wall. There were times when they seemed to inch ahead, and often it was necessary to backtrack and find a way around some obstacle. Fred was leading again, glad this time to have Sessions riding with him to choose the most likely way.

The dangers of the Moon appeared more real here. In spite of this, there was a strange beauty to this world. The sharp rock faces were often colored by minerals, and the glare of the sun overhead was reflected and re-reflected from rock to rock, softening the shadows until it was hard to believe there was no air to diffuse the light. Most of the surface was dulled and grayed from the constant bombarding by solar particles and radiation, but there was a beauty to the Moon totally unlike anything on Earth.

They were near the top of a mountain range at lunchtime, but they had run into a point where Sessions felt it better to send men on foot ahead to spot the trail. They found a way leading along a rock ledge barely wide enough to hold the tractors, with a thousand-foot drop below. The ledge was covered with broken shards that had to be cleared away to prevent the tractors slipping. Fred didn't envy the two men Sessions chose for the job.

At the end of the day, with the descent barely begun, they stopped at the first safe place. Fred pointed out through the side port of the tractor. "From up here, it isn't hard to see where we should have come. See— down there, through that gorge?"

Sessions held up his map. He'd already marked off the trail for the return trip.

It took another day to get through the mountains. They were beginning to fall behind schedule, but they expected to make better time in the flatter areas. However, a new phenomenon appeared: something like a low mist over the flats. To Fred's surprise, his viewing ports slowly began to grow murky, as if something were settling on them.

The drivers and Sessions stopped and found it was dust. Sessions seemed unsurprised as he discussed it with Ruth Miles, the expedition astronomer.

Nobody had found a large area covered with the dust before, but astronomers had predicted it; it had been observed as a false "atmosphere" for radar signals. The dust was so fine that it picked up a charge from the solar particles which struck the surface—the same particles causing the Van Allen belts around Earth. Since any two bodies having the same charge tend to repel each other, the dust grains moved apart. They were so fine that the charge lifted them off the surface of the Moon and formed what seemed to be a mist.

"What created all the dust here?" Fred asked. There was no action of wind and rain to wear away the rocks.

"I haven't any idea. Maybe expansion and cooling between day and night temperature extremes." Sessions shook his head. "It is finer than I'd expect it to be from that, however. We'll take samples and let the experts on Earth figure out what they can. We should run a voltage gradient check to determine the charge, too."

The dancing dust made it harder to see the ground, forcing them to go more slowly. Everything was all right for the rest of the day. It wasn't until the following day that they came to a great fissure that split the flat territory apart. It was far too wide and deep to cross, and it stretched as far as they could see. The maps drawn from the photographs showed no sign of it. Apparently it had been masked by the dust.

There was no way of being sure of the best direction, but the crevasse seemed to grow slightly narrower toward the north, so they turned right. The most they could hope for was that it would prove fairly short.

In that, their hopes were false. Two days were spent following the great split before it finally came to an abrupt end, the crack narrowing from its full width to nothing in only a mile or so. Then they turned west again and tried to make up for lost time. Now, however, the sun was sinking nearer the horizon, lengthening the shadows and glaring through the filters over the ports.

They were moving at a cautious five miles an hour when Fred felt the nose of the tractor jerk downward abruptly. His hands shoved the controls, stopping the tracks and spinning them backward violently, but it was too late. The headquarters trailer behind bumped him forward, to be followed by a smaller bump from the supply trailer. The tractor slid forward and down at a 45-degree angle before he could stop it.

Fortunately, the air lock was in the rear. He snapped

on his helmet and was outside, just as Sessions and several men from the other tractors came up to him. From the ground, it was easy to see that the tractor had broken through a thin crust into an underground hole.

"Good work, Fred," Sessions said over the intersuit radio. "A fraction of a second slower response and you'd have gone in. Think you can back out if we get the trailers out of the way?"

Fred remembered the lack of response from the tracks. "I think you'd better pull me out with another tractor," he decided, glad to see quick approval from the leader.

It proved to be nothing serious, though it wasted time. In another hour, they were moving ahead again, reducing speed still further in case they encountered other faults in the surface. There was no way to detect them in advance. It was one more risk the expedition had to take.

The next two days were uneventful, though the dust got thicker as they reached the bottom of the great plain. When the sun sank lower, however, the dust began to sink back toward the surface, drifting into the hollows. Apparently there were no longer enough charged particles reaching the surface to maintain the repulsion. Sometimes the tracks of the tractor threw the dust up from small hollows. At other times, the stuff was so fine that it behaved almost like a lubricant under the tracks, making them slip.

Fred wasn't startled later when the tractor began slipping at an angle. Suddenly he realized it was actually moving sideways, as if sliding down a steep incline. He threw power on, putting more on one track than the other. The response was slow at first, but it began to right the machine's movements and for a second, bring it away from the slip; a moment later, the sideways lurch was more pronounced.

Again he stepped up the power until the motor was hissing at its maximum. The right tread spun wildly, caught, then spun again. This time the tractor slewed around and began climbing out of the dust.

The mirror showed worse news, though. The big trailer was also sliding sideways, deeper into the dust. Sessions, riding in the lead tractor again, noticed it at the same time and motioned for more speed, but the motor was already doing its best.

Then the treads bit and sent the tractor lurching forward. The trailer skidded further and started to sink.

Suddenly the big hitch that connected tractor to trailer snapped apart under the strain.

The trailer went on skidding to the right and away from the tractor. As they watched, it sank deeper and deeper.

By the time the two men could get through the tractor's air lock, the roof of the trailer had vanished completely under the dust, carrying their most important instruments and several of the men with it.

CHAPTER 8 /

Dust Trap

MOST OF the other men from the expedition were piling out of the trailers and gathering around to stare at the place where the laboratory trailer had sunk. Sessions waved them back, giving instructions over his radio.

"The men inside the laboratory are perfectly safe, if that pit isn't too deep, and there's nothing most of you can do. Unless you have some specific ideas to help, go back to your regular places." He studied the ground with care as the others drew back reluctantly. "It can't be more than a couple hundred feet across the dust pocket—you can see rocks over there that must be close to the surface. I suppose we can probe with rods to locate the trailer."

"I could try going down after it and attaching a cable to the hitch," Fred offered.

The dust behaved like quicksand, only its action was much faster. It was as fine as the best grade of talcum, almost like a liquid in its ability to give under pressure. A man in a spacesuit should be safe in it unless the slope leading down under it was too steep for him to return.

Two of the other men who had been listening now came up to Sessions. "Better let us do it, sir," Mike Boland suggested. "Dr. Wallace and I both had experience at the South Pole, and this is a lot like losing one of the sleds in a snow pocket."

Fred recognized the wisdom of it, even before Sessions agreed. He went to one of the big lockers along the side of the tractor and began removing a length of cable that could be hitched to the trailer. He had just uncoiled it when a shout over the radio made him swing around.

There was a little stirring in the dust, and the antenna tip of the buried trailer poked up. At its full extension, it was about two feet above the dust level.

Mona Williams' voice sounded faintly in his headphones. "Everybody all right down here. Am I reaching you?"

The dust was grounding the signal enough to weaken it. While Sessions answered, Fred grinned in reluctant admiration at the tone of her words. The girl seemed completely unafraid; her voice held only impatience and annoyance.

Now that they had a clear idea of the location of the trailer and the depth of the dust trap, the work was greatly simplified. An examination of the broken hitch on the tractor showed that it would have to be replaced.

"You'll have to install it by feel, I guess," Fred told Boland and Wallace. The dust would blind them and make lights useless.

Inside the helmet, Boland's dark, wide face split into an easy grin. "No worse than working in some of the blizzards we've seen. Got tools here, Halpern?"

The two men took the tools, replacement hitch, and the cable and headed into the dust pit, feeling for the hard surface ahead with sections of welding rod. As they moved forward, they sank slowly until their heads disappeared. The cable snaked out, showing they were making progress. Then it remained still for a few moments, until a double jerk indicated the men had found the front of the trailer.

Judging by the antenna, Fred backed the tractor into position, getting as close to the dust trap as he dared. He went out again, to start work on its fractured hitch.

Sessions joined him, watching the operation between glances at the dust pit. The scientist took the part Fred removed and examined it. "This was defective, Fred. See how the fracture runs? It's a good thing it didn't break back on that ledge in the mountains. And there's no way of testing the other hitches."

Fred was shaken. The flaw had been too deep for discovery at Emmett Base, but all the metal parts supposedly had been inspected for hidden faults before leaving Earth. Some man in a testing operation had been a little careless, unaware of how important the checks were. The accident could have taken several lives.

"I'm beginning to see why discipline and responsibility are necessary," he muttered.

Sessions grinned. "I didn't mean to point a finger at you, Fred. But you're right. Ah!"

The cable had given three jerks, which meant the job was done. Fred drew it taut and began fastening it to the new hitch. He finished just as Boland and Wallace came out of the pit, guiding themselves along the cable.

It was not difficult to get the trailer out now, though he urged the tractor ahead at minimum speed until he could see the wheels of the trailer break free. He went on a few feet more before stopping and going back to examine the trailer for damage. Together with Sessions and the ones who had been inside, he went over every inch of it. There was no sign of damage, and the dust seemed to have slipped off completely.

He touched his helmet to that of Mona Williams while they stood side by side. Sound could pass from helmet to helmet without the use of radio. "That was smart thinking to raise the antenna."

"Thanks," she said tersely; there was no warmth in her voice. He couldn't see her face, and a second later she was moving away.

They picked up the trail again, moving slowly through the thick dust. The treads of the tractor sent up great whorls of it. It drifted back slowly under the weak lunar gravitation; since there was no air to keep it from falling, it settled before the next tractor reached the same spot.

During the next day, they hunted their way through a section of broken boulders that seemed to cross the plain, then ran into more of the huge dust bowl. There was still a range of cliffs and mountains ahead of them before they could reach their destination.

Fred began noticing a queer sound as another day passed. It wasn't steady, and sometimes was missing for hours. But each time it returned, it was worse. He went over the undercarriage of the tractor during the next lunch break, and could find nothing. It was back as they took up the trail again, coming for longer intervals, with shorter breaks. It was a thumping that seemed to be transmitted through the floor of the tractor. He tried to spot its location, but the whole floor acted as a sounding board, making it impossible to find the origin of the trouble below him.

He called Sessions over the radio, and the leader joined him. The sound was stronger now. The scientist glanced at his watch. "Want to stop and hunt for it, Fred, or do you think we can trust the machinery for another hour? We'll be halting at the base of the mountains then."

That would take them further out of the dust, probably into an area high enough to be free of the stuff entirely, making inspection easier. They decided to go on.

After dinner, Sessions sent Boland to help Fred look for the trouble. The man was listed as a highly specialized type of mineralogist, but his work required using so much heavy equipment that he claimed to be a good mechanic as well. Most of the men on the expedition had been picked for a diversity of abilities.

Working together, they managed to jack up one side of the tractor and get one of the treads and shields off. Then they examined the complicated machinery that powered and guided the big silicone rubber treads over a series of rollers.

The sun had dropped below the horizon in the west, and they were working by artificial light. That was an advantage over the uncontrollable sunlight for this purpose. The ground was cooling; it would soon be far below freezing, sinking hundreds of degrees below zero before the long lunar night ended. This was another advantage to the work; the suits could be warmed by battery power much more easily than they could be kept insulated from the high daytime heat.

"Dust in everything," Fred commented as they worked. "It must have worked its way into the grease fittings. I'll try forcing the old silicone grease out with a new pressure dose. Find anything, Mike?"

The heavily built man wriggled further forward. "Nothing yet. I don't like the looks of a lot of this, Fred, but it's just a feeling I get. Sure the motor bearings are sound?"

"The motor's behaving," Fred answered. That was one area where he was the expert, and he'd been over it thoroughly.

Boland grunted suddenly. "Here. Come take a look."

It was a bearing on one of the differential shafts. As Fred felt it, he could see it move slightly, indicating wear that created enough play to let the shaft whip, accounting for the sounds he had heard. Naturally, it was one of the hardest bearings to get out, and one for which there was no replacement. He crawled back for more tools, grumbling with Boland as they went to work on it. They would have to take it off, smooth down the shaft, and pour Babbitt metal to form a new bearing face in the old part. It was makeshift, but the best they could do. The whole operation took more than four hours.

They skirted along the plain the next day, looking for a pass through the mountain chain. It was nearly hopeless in the dark, since their most powerful lights could not reveal enough details to show how far any trail went. The route suggested by the photographs had proved impossible; a two-hundred-foot cliff blocked their way, although it was not in the picture.

The original schedule called for passage through the mountains during the period of lunar day, but their progress had fallen far behind. Now they might have to run three hundred miles north and double back to get around the mountains, rather than blindly attempting to go through.

It wasn't all bad, however. Driving by the beams of the powerful lights was easier than heading into the sun. "Beams," of course, was not quite the right word; there was no air to show the path of light, which simply reflected back from whatever it struck. Seeing was nearly perfect within the range of the lights.

"I read a story once in some magazine about animals living here," Ruth Miles said the next evening. "The author had it figured out that the beasts lived on the run, going around their world and staying near sunset, where it wasn't too hot."

"That would be some running, aside from live animals being impossible here," one of the men objected.

Fred had been computing it in his head. The tables had been lifted to the ceiling and they were dropping the shelflike bunks from the walls, getting ready to turn in. "It wouldn't require too much speed. The terminator between light and dark moves about ten miles an hour here at the Moon's equator, instead of a thousand as it does on Earth. In this gravity, that wouldn't be hard."

"I guess I read the same story," Dr. Villiers, the biologist, said. He sounded wistful. "There were supposed to be plants that built oxygen domes for the animals to live on. Not a bad idea, even if it wasn't true. I wish there were some life here—any kind. It would be the biggest discovery since fire."

They batted the idea around, getting nowhere with it. Fred realized he was being accepted finally as one of them. Perhaps time was partly responsible; he suspected the closer contact with Boland had helped, for Boland was well liked by everyone else. There were still lingering doubts about him, he supposed. However, the men seemed willing to be convinced.

Then the tractor began to make noises again. This time, the sounds were different and equally disturbing. Something was under the tractor and Fred and Boland investigated. Although the new bearing wasn't perfect, it was holding up fairly well, and they could probably renew it. Others were showing signs of wear, though. Apparently they had been unable to get all of the dust out of the grease supply.

"It might not matter too much," Boland summed up their conclusions for Dr. Sessions. "It only takes a little wear to make some machinery noisy. That doesn't mean it's ready for the scrap heap. I vote that it's still safe enough."

They went on, but the next day things were worse. On the twelfth day out from Base, the whining and muttering sounds changed to a clatter which could mean more serious trouble.

Sessions worked with them that night, holding the light and trying to be helpful. The expedition was his responsibility, and his reason for being there was the need to see the damage for himself. Others might know more about machinery, but he wanted his own impressions.

The original repair was about half worn, but the damage was less serious than Fred had thought. Other signs of wear were showing up. The injection of new silicone grease under pressure couldn't free tiny particles of dust ground into the metal or caked in the old grease.

The chief cause of the new sound was a shaft which must have bound in its bearing and twisted under the strain of torque. It was slightly bent, though it had worn free in the bearing; at each rotation it set up an imbalance that was transmitted to other parts of the under-carriage. There was no way of being sure how much the distortion had weakened it.

Sessions crawled under the tractor, studying things while they explained what they had found. His face was grim as he came out with them and watched as they made what temporary repairs they could. There wasn't too much to be done.

In the morning, everyone was called together in the trailer that served as the men's bunkroom. They huddled together, sitting on the bunks, while Sessions summed up the situation, with some explanations from Fred and Boland.

It wasn't a pretty picture. There were parts that needed dust shields to prevent further trouble on the plains where they were headed. Such things should have been installed originally, but nobody had realized that the old theory of the dancing dust would prove to be fact; the first few flat areas explored were ones where no dust had formed, though false radar indications probably proved that there were far more dust-ridden sections than had been believed since men first reached the Moon. The grease fittings also needed tighter sealing, and seals should be provided at opposite ends.

As a result of wear, there were a number of major bearings which needed proper relining, rather than a temporary job of pouring in babbitt. Some of the shafts were roughened; they could be smoothed down with files and crocus cloth, but a true finish took better machinery. Finally, there were other major replacements or repairs, and the whole drive mechanism of the tractors needed rigid inspection.

"Funny all those things keep happening to Fred's tractor," one of the men remarked. A few faces looked startled and then speculative.

"That's enough!" Sessions said sharply. "Mr. Halpern has been in the lead most of the time. I've assigned him the toughest job, and it isn't at all surprising that his machine shows more damage than the others."

He went back to his summation. In his judgment there wasn't enough they could do here to insure safety. The tractor needed to be taken back to the ships, where more equipment for repairs was available, or to be worked on in the shop of the colonists. While the other tractors seemed to be standing up, they could no longer be trusted without a thorough going-over.

The only solution was to turn back. They could leave the laboratory and supply trailers behind in a cache here, to be picked up again on the next trip. Traveling light, they would make much better time with the advantage of knowing the trail.

Someone suggested leaving the dormitory trailers, but Sessions vetoed that at once.

"Nobody stays behind. I won't risk having men stranded here because of some accident happening to our tractors. The equipment can be lost—but no lives, if I can help it."

They began unloading at once, setting up a plastic tent to hold the supplies not required on the short return trip. The tractors pulled the small supply trailers and the laboratory into a square around it. They installed an automatic radio responder beacon on the cache, set to start transmitting upon being triggered by a coded pulse from one of the radios. It would guarantee their finding the cache, even if they lost directions somewhere on the trip back.

Mike Boland touched helmets with Fred. "Forget that nonsense spouted back there, Fred," he said. "There's always some sorehead in any group. Most of the guys know that you've had the trouble because you've had the rough job of leading."

Fred muttered his thanks. He had been trying to forget the accusation that he was responsible for the trouble. For that matter, the man who'd spoken against him might not have meant the words; boredom and frustration over the wasted time on the trail had shortened tempers.

The words had been said, nevertheless, and the idea planted. These men weren't superstitious, yet they knew that some people really were accident prone; it wouldn't take many disappointments to convince them that he was such a modern jinx. After that, working with them would be nearly impossible for Fred.

The worst part of it was that he couldn't be entirely sure in his own mind that he wasn't an accident prone—too many things had gone wrong around him.

CHAPTER 9/

Rock Slide

TRAVELING LIGHT, they made much better time than had been possible on the trip out. The darkness helped in many ways, too. The dust settled as soon as the charge of particles from the sun vanished; this made it easier to tell what kind of ground they were covering. They soon learned to spot dust pits by the extreme smoothness of the dust.

Fred was in the lead again. Although his tractor had suffered the most damage, it was now traveling without a trailer. There was too much noise from the worn parts, but no sign that things were getting worse. He cut straight across the level plain toward the mountain passage they had left days before.

They made a brief stop for lunch, while Dr. Sessions beamed a tight radio signal out toward space and the Station circling Earth. Since there was no air on the Moon, radio signals could not be reflected below the horizon, thus there was no way to reach Emmett Base directly; the Station would pick up the message and relay it to Base, so that everything would be ready by the time the expedition returned.

There was another stop for dinner, then Dr. Sessions decided to push straight on, without the usual halt for sleep.

"I don't like continuous driving," he told Fred. "But

we've lost too much time on this trip already. Can you handle a twelve-hour shift in the lead, Fred?"

Fred nodded. It wasn't hard physical work, though it required constant alertness. With the breaks for lunch and dinner, he would have enough rest to handle it. "Mike Boland knows how to drive the tractor," he suggested.

"I already told him he'd be your relief," Sessions said, breaking into a quick smile. He went off to talk with the other drivers, appointing reliefs for each.

Fred rode with Boland for about an hour, making sure that the geologist picked up all the hints and tricks he had learned in judging the land over which they traveled. Then he bunked down in the dormitory trailer. It took a little while to get used to its pitching and bumping motion, but he was tired enough to fall asleep without much trouble.

The next day, one of the other tractors reported trouble with the drive train, and the third reported similar trouble in another hour. Inspection at the next lunch stop showed wear, but no evidence that the machines couldn't make the trip back. They pushed on.

This time, they took the alternate passage through the mountains which they had spotted on the trip out. It was a risk; the pass could have difficulties no one could see from above, and finding alternate trails in the darkness would be a problem. The risk seemed justified, for the old passage had been too tricky and had taken too much time. As it turned out, the new pass had only one really bad place—a break caused by a rock slide. After careful examination, they found a way around which took less than an hour. Boland shook his head in amazement as the miles of the passage went by without serious trouble.

"This stuff looks as if an ancient lava flow had filled in a deep cut along here to make a road for us. There wasn't supposed to be that much volcanic activity on the Moon. I wonder if we'll ever really understand how any of the planets and satellites were formed."

"We still haven't explored much distance beyond Base," Fred reminded him. "We can't learn everything in a few weeks."

Boland laughed. "Fred, it's tougher than you think. We've been studying Earth scientifically for two centuries now, and we still don't know much about our own planet. In fact, we've learned almost as much about her from these Moon expeditions as we learned in all our other efforts. It would take hundreds of explorations to get any real idea of what this little world is like. Remind me to show you something after dinner, if the weather reports for Earth were right."

Fred didn't have to remind him, and the weather reports had been right, of course; from the Station, predicting major weather a month ahead was not difficult. Boland came up, carrying a small six-power telescope. "Come away from the lights of the trailers," he suggested. "Back behind one of those rocks."

Once they were in darkness, Earth was a majestic sight in the sky. Four times as large as the Moon when seen from Earth, the bluish-green tint and the markings of oceans and continents showing through the white clouds were a sight to lift anyone's heart. It seemed like a great jewel resting on black velvet, with a thick sprinkle of stars to give it a setting. The atmosphere of the planet gave it a soft mantle.

Part of Europe, the Mediterranean Sea, and much of Africa were visible, and the clouds seemed to have vanished from most of the atmosphere above them. It was one of the times when the surface could be seen clearly. Fred took the telescope and began studying his home world. He'd seen it often enough from the Station, where it seemed to fill most of the sky, but this view was somehow entirely different.

Abruptly he gasped. Uncertain and hard to see at first, there were hints of lines that made a network across the land masses. The lines seemed to run for hundreds of miles in straight sweeps that might have been made by a ruler. Some were double, and one appeared to be triple. Where the lines met, there were spots of larger size, like nodes from which the criss-crossing lines spread out.

"Canals!" he said.

Boland laughed. "That's what the astronomers called them when they saw those lines on Mars. Or they called them *canali*—channels. People used to argue whether they were really there or just optical illusions. They seemed to show up to the eye but not on photographs taken of Mars."

"What are they, Mike?"

"We just don't know." Boland's voice was hushed, yet oddly excited. "Fred, I have no idea. The best satellite photos show nothing at all where they seem to be, either on Earth or Mars. And there's nothing on the surface to account for them. They aren't canals, channels or even cracks in the ground. Yet under the right conditions, they show up to the eye—and most observers see them in the same positions, though some people see more of them than others."

"Then they really are just optical illusions?" Fred asked.

"Probably. But they don't show up on the Moon when seen from Earth. There's a theory held by a few scientists that those *canali* are somehow related to the magnetic field of a planet—and the Moon has no magnetic field. There's also some indication that plants grow best on Earth where the lines and nodes lie. But so far, the more we learn, the less we know. It's a mysterious universe—and a wonderful one. Come on, let's get back to camp."

Fred's tractor was limping badly when they reached Emmett Base. The last hundred miles had been traveled at reduced speed. It had been a much shorter trip than the one out, and it was only the seventeenth day from their original departure.

It was a relief to turn the tractor over to the repair group and the colonists. After the steady driving and the strain of expecting a breakdown at any moment, Fred was tired. He didn't realize how tired until he could afford at last to let down and relax. He slept for twelve straight hours and woke up ravenously hungry. He was rested, but with the let-down feeling that follows a long stretch of tension.

Jonas found him a few minutes later. "Hi, Fred. I'm going out to the mine, and Sessions thought you might like to come along. Want to try the hike?"

"Hike?" Fred asked. He knew that the mine lay some thirty miles away from Base. Then he laughed at his own habits of thought. That wasn't too bad a trip on the Moon. A man could keep up a trot that carried him along at more than ten miles an hour; in this gravity, man and suit together weighed only sixty or seventy pounds.

He fell in beside the older man, and they headed out along a well-worn trail. "We used to haul people back and forth by one of our three tractors," Jonas said. "But now we're forced to use them full time at the mines. Even three are barely enough to do the work we have to finish. I'll be glad when your expedition goes back and leaves us those improved models you've been driving."

The steady trot was no more fatiguing than walking would have been on Earth, and Jonas kept up a stream of conversation. He knew most of what had happened on the expedition, and there was little new in the colony. However, the regular news from Earth was filled with speculations that might be important to the Moon.

Most of the news centered around something Fred's father was planning, though nobody knew for sure what it might be. Apparently Congress was worried about hints that it involved the Moon and probably Dr. Ramachundra. Space was supposed to be international, but most of the people at Emmett Base were from the United States, and Congress sometimes acted as if the Base were a part of America. There had always been a small element in the Government—just as there was among the people—that objected to any new idea about space. These people would protest violently against letting the World Congress send Ramachundra to investigate the colony. A few Representatives were demanding that Colonel Halpern be replaced.

"Must have something to do with the new spaceship," Jonas said. "At least there's editorial pressure to bring it back to Earth and complete the tests there. But Wickman's still at the Station, and so is Ramachundra. Maybe your father has figured how to get him here. Wish I knew how much good that would do."

Fred found very little in the rumors that was convincing. The colonists grasped at every hope, however vague, which probably explained the speculations. The one part that seemed to have any truth to it was that his father was about to go through an annoying investigation of his running of the Station. Fred felt sure Colonel Halpern could stand that; nobody had ever found anything in his work that couldn't stand up to criticism.

When they reached the mines, Fred was beginning to feel the strain of the steady pace, but interest and curiosity soon overcame his fatigue.

The mine was actually nothing but a deep pit. It had been found in an area where a small crater had been created by a meteoric collision; the miners had dug in even deeper along one wall. This was the only source of copper that had been located on the Moon. Copper was valuable because it could be worked easily and made the best available electrical conductor.

There were about thirty men working the mine, using crude equipment. Two small smelters handled the ore, heating it by electrical current from an arrangement of solar mirrors. These were not working now, since the sun was down. The whole area was bathed in artificial light, and Fred could see that the men were digging out more ore and getting ready for the time when the smelters could be used again.

A figure in a spacesuit waved and came over at a fast trot, sticking out a hand. "Freddy. It's good to see you."

It took some seconds to recognize the man as Jim Stanley, who had first taught Fred how to handle himself in space. Stanley had developed and matured remarkably in four years. Now, Fred gathered, he was in charge of the entire mine. They had a few minutes together before some signal from below drew Stanley away. Jonas started after him, but turned back for a moment.

"You'll get a better view from up here, so maybe you'd better look the place over before coming down," he suggested. "I'll be free in half an hour. We can look into things then."

Jonas and Stanley went down a crude elevator. It was suspended from a frail arrangement of metal struts that stuck out over the small cliff. A platform was suspended on a pulley, counterbalanced by a heavy weight, and worked by manpower. It didn't look any too substantial, and Fred saw that the operator at the top of the cliff was busy repairing one of the struts.

Most of what went on was difficult to understand, though he could follow the basic idea of digging out the ore. The tractors were serving as bulldozers, heavy movers, and general power-sources. He saw two of them busy moving rubble out of the way to open up a new vein, but the third was not visible.

Then he saw it, at the top of the cliff, further along the ledge on which he stood. The tractor was stopped, but it must have been making a wider break in the sloping walls above it, probably to form a new road for carrying material back to Base. As he looked, he saw the operator and another man moving back from it, making gestures as if they were in some kind of argument. Since they were using direct contact instead of radio, the gestures meant nothing. After a minute more of argument, they both headed toward a group of diggers further away.

Fred joined the elevator operator. "Anything I can do?"

"Not much." The voice was a woman's. In the suits, it was often hard to tell men and women apart. "I don't like the way this shackle is wiggling, but it seems strong enough. I'll have a welder look at it after this shift."

Fred could see nothing wrong, but it was outside his experience. He stared out at the pit again. "What about your source of iron?"

She laughed. "You're looking at it!" Then her voice sobered. "This is one of the few pieces of good luck we've had. The meteor that hit here was a nickel-iron one. We dug in originally to get it, and found the copper ore by lucky accident. By the way, I'm Helva Peterson."

By following the signs Helva pointed out, Fred could just see the shaft down to the meteorite. The presence of such a supply of metal explained how they were able to smelt iron without more power than they seemed to possess. With the pure metal from space, no such smelting would be needed. Still, it must involve a tremendous amount of work. The stuff was a high-grade steel in its natural form—in fact, the first steel men discovered probably came from small meteorites that fell on Earth. This steel would be incredibly hard to cut into sizes that could be forged into usable parts.

Fred felt sure, however, that someone had told him all the iron on the Moon came from low-grade ore.

Helva nodded at his question. "At first, we did have to smelt a little. The old mine is further out. But when this was located, we gave that up."

She turned at a signal from below which Fred hadn't noticed. Someone wanted to come up. Fred moved forward to help her operate the crank that raised the little platform, but she motioned him away.

"It isn't so hard," she assured him. "Besides, I'm used to it, and with that shackle, I don't want any strain added. It takes time to get the feel of running this smoothly."

It made sense, and Fred got back out of the way. From up here, he could see nothing of the rising platform, but the supporting structure tilted outward slightly as weight was added to it. Helva bent to the winch. The elevator seemed geared to rise about one foot for each full turn of the crank.

It couldn't have been more than the first foot above the bottom when the accident happened. The shackle must have come loose. The strut it held whipped wildly backward.

Helva felt the action and stepped back to avoid it, but not quite fast enough. The ragged edge of broken metal caught against the side of her suit, ripping a gash a foot long. Air rushed out, the moisture in it freezing as it expanded. She grabbed at the cut, her face horrified as the pressure in her suit sank to nothing.

Fred leaped forward and caught her. The rip was too large to patch there; his hand secured the open edges, twisting them together to cut down the leakage, while he yanked the oxygen valve on her helmet all the way open. It would give her two or three minutes more air. After that, unless she were inside an air chamber, she'd suffocate.

He caught sight of the tractor. It was the only possible place to carry her. Fred's hands swung her over his shoulder, still holding the torn edge, and he ran. He could cover the distance in a minute and get her through the lock in no more time. It was the only chance.

Fortunately, the outer lock was open. He leaped inside, carrying the girl, and snapped it shut, without waiting for the lock to fill with air; it was faster to force through the inner lock. He unfastened it, hitting it with his shoulder. Pressure inside resisted, until some air had run into the lock. Then the inner seal gave suddenly, and they slammed through. The force of his thrust sent him reeling forward, to be brought up with a crash against the control panel at the front of the cabin.

Abruptly, the little tractor seemed to sag under him. The nose dipped, the treads squeaked through the floor, and the machine began to slip.

He scarcely had time to realize that the tractor was tilting over the edge of the cliff before they went hurtling to the pit floor, sixty feet below.

CHAPTER 10 /

Pariah

SIXTY FEET on the Moon was no worse than ten on Earth. The fall lasted for nearly five seconds in the low gravity, giving Fred time to remember this. He pulled Helva down onto the operator's seat and braced himself against it to take the shock of impact when they landed.

They hit bottom with a sickening crash. With a shrieking and ripping of metal, the tractor struck undercarriage down. Fred felt his knees buckle and pitched to the floor. His stomach felt as if he had been kicked. Then the tractor settled onto the floor of the pit.

He got to his feet, shaken, but with no broken bones. The seat had cushioned Helva on deep springs; she was unconscious, but that was probably from the minutes during which she'd had insufficient oxygen. He drew off her helmet, then turned to inspect the damage.

Surprisingly, the tractor body hadn't been much hurt. One corner was dented inward badly, but there was no tear in the metal, and no sound of air rushing out. That had been the greatest danger; Fred began to breathe more easily.

In another minute, there was the sound of the air lock, which still worked. Apparently the back end of the tractor cabin hadn't been damaged by the landing. A spacesuited man came through, carrying a suit and oxygen bottle.

Helva was already sitting up, beginning to gasp as her

lungs sucked in air. The man tossed her the spacesuit, slipping back his helmet.

"I saw the whole thing," he said. "You were lucky, I guess." He filled in the rough details for Helva, who had been unconscious during the entire crash— mercifully, for it had left her fully relaxed and better able to take the rough landing.

"The tractor?" she asked.

The man shook his head in grim silence. He waited until she changed suits, making sure the strut hadn't injured her—it had merely touched the suit—and motioned them out.

Fred followed, just beginning to realize what this accident must mean to them. "The driver of this . . ." he began.

"Yeah," the other man said. "He felt the tractor slipping and came back here to get help in pulling it back to safety. That's why it was abandoned. I guess you couldn't know that or help what you did."

They found everyone from the pit grouped around as they came out. No examination of the tractor was necessary. It had landed on a hummock, striking first where the motor was located. That had absorbed most of the shock. Now the motor was a hopeless wreck, flattened and crumpled beyond repair. The drive and tread structure was smashed so badly that it could never be put back in working order. The tractor was ruined permanently. With it went one-third of the most important equipment of the colony.

Nobody seemed to blame Fred. The miners went out of their way to admit that he couldn't have known about the tractor, and that he would have had to save Helva in any event. But they couldn't be cheerful about the tragedy.

Helva touched helmets briefly. "Thank you for saving my life, Mr. Halpern," she said. Her voice showed that she'd rather have been killed than to be saved at such a high cost to her friends and the future of the Moon.

Fred stayed out of sight as much as he could until Jonas was ready to return. There was nothing he could do to help them. Nobody blamed him, yet things went wrong too often when he was around.

Jonas tried to cheer him up on the return trip, hours later, but even he seemed depressed.

There, Fred thought, went his last chance to find a future in space. He'd held on to the idea that when the expedition was over he might be able to stay here, rather than go back to the Station—and from there to Earth forever. He'd done everything he could to prove himself a man they could use here on the Moon. Now there would be no further chance to convince everybody he wasn't more of a menace than they had feared.

In the Administration hut, Gantry listened to the account with a flat, unemotional expression. When it was finished, he sighed and turned to Fred.

"You did the right thing," he said quietly. "Don't blame yourself, because I'm not going to blame you for it. You used the best judgment you could—better than many of us could have used in the time you had—and that's all I ask of any man. So forget it."

"Thanks, Governor Gantry. But will anyone else really forget it?"

"No." Gantry sighed again. "No, you're right, Fred. You'll be a pariah here, unfortunately. That's the way people are, I'm sorry to say. They know it's nothing you could help, but down inside their emotions, they'll avoid contact with you like the plague. I'm afraid we haven't changed much since the sailors threw Jonah overboard because they thought he brought bad luck."

It was the same conclusion Fred had reached. He couldn't even resent the fact that he'd become a pariah, a symbol of bad luck; with the troubles the colonists were having, it was a wonder any of them could remain sane and normal at all.

He felt bitter about the reaction of the men of the expedition, though. They had no real reason for their attitude, but news of the accident increased their hostility. He had seen Mona Williams talking to a couple of the others and looking his way when he wasn't supposed to notice. That kind of petty viciousness hurt worse than the honest reaction of the colonists. He noticed that she was careful whenever Dr. Sessions was around, however.

The next day there was work for him to do repairing the expedition's tractors. He made sure he would be able to work without having to go into the colony, then joined Boland and a few others. It was a hard, worrisome job, and it took some of his thoughts away from his own problems. There was also satisfaction in doing something he knew was useful.

There were too few spare parts, and the tools carried on the ships for their own repair and maintenance were inadequate. Some of the work had to be done in the tool-shop of the colony, using precious supplies from their meager surplus. But under the drive of necessity, things were being managed.

To Fred's surprise, even Poorhouse came out and pitched in. The pilot was as good a mechanic as Boland, and better than Fred. It occurred to Fred that the rule against pilots doing other work might make sense; they depended on a hairline balance of coördination to operate the ships. That couldn't be maintained if they were annoyed by outside requirements. Most of them felt just as strongly about the need to explore space as any man on the expedition, so perhaps they even resented the regulation against other work they had been forced to insist on.

Fred was beginning to worry about his father. He heard a few of the news broadcasts beamed to the Base, and they didn't sound encouraging. Politics had never interested him; he couldn't untangle its complicated threads. Yet he sensed there was a struggle going on between two groups, catching his father between the two as in the jaws of a vise.

He asked Dr. Sessions, and was immediately granted permission to put a call through to his father. There was little to report on the expedition, and no reason why a few minutes at the ship transmitter couldn't be turned over to him. At the other end, Colonel Halpern was far less available; Fred had to wait nearly half an hour before his father's voice came over the speaker.

It was a tired voice, yet with an undernote of genuine pleasure in it. "Glad you could call me, son. Dr. Sessions reports you're doing fine."

There was always a lag of seconds between the ends of a conversation across space; radio, like light, traveled only 186,000 miles a second, and the Station was about 250,000 miles away. It made awkward pauses, but it was something to which the speakers soon became accustomed.

Fred reported a few of the things he'd done. Then he asked the question he most wanted answered. "How are things with you, Dad?"

He must have managed to get his real meaning into his tone of voice, for his father laughed suddenly.

"Freddy, things are a mess. But don't believe half of what you hear. I don't think they'll be able to kick me out of command for a while. By the time they can, it may be too late."

In spite of the rumors and hints in the news, Fred had never seriously considered that anyone might want to remove his father from command; that Colonel Halpern would mention it made it suddenly seem real. Things must be coming to a head, but there was no chance to discuss the situation. His father dropped the subject and began passing on messages from others on the Station—seemingly needless messages—until Fred realized with the final one that there was a point to it.

"Oh, yes. Major Wickman sends you his regards. He

says he'll look you up the first chance he gets. I never knew you two felt so close."

Fred grinned slowly. "We're both members of a little club called the Moon-boys," he answered.

The laughter at the other end was well rehearsed. It almost masked the sudden relaxing in Colonel Halpern's voice as he realized his message had been properly interpreted. "Okay, son. Take care of yourself."

"You, too, Dad," Fred said with more feeling than he'd meant to put in it.

He realized as the official messages resumed that he and his father were actually closer in some ways across all this space than they had ever been when face to face. Maybe it was because they couldn't see each other, and weren't as afraid of their emotions.

Certainly his father never had tried to let him know what seemed to be secret information before. That was the only possible interpretation to the message. Wickman must be getting ready to make a flight to the Moon, since that was the only way he could "look up" Fred. The laughter at the idea of Wickman also being a "Moon-boy" confirmed it.

Fred couldn't see that it would do any good to send the *Cosmic Egg* on such a voyage. There must be far more going on than he guessed. For a moment the old resentment rose in him. If this was important, it meant Wickman would be doing the things Fred had always hoped to find himself doing. Why Wickman?

He put the idea out of his mind and went to the edge of the cliff to look down at the Administration hut. It was the time when the colony would be sleeping, but Gantry often stayed up far longer than most of the others. Fred knew this was his best chance to find the Governor alone. He headed down the crude stone stairs, toward the hut.

Gantry was there, astonished to see Fred. He listened while the young man reported the conversation with his father. Fred would have liked to believe that the message was a personal one from his father, but he realized it was only a means of getting word to the colony in a manner which wouldn't leak back to Earth.

"I don't know," Gantry said, when Fred finished. "Thanks for bringing the news, Fred. I must say it doesn't mean much to me. Oh, I know rumors are going around. I've heard too many rumors, usually about things that had nothing to do with us. Whenever men live on nothing but hope, you'll always find rumors."

"You probably know what it means more than I do," Fred protested.

Gantry nodded. "Maybe. I know there are some people who have wanted to do anything they could to help us. Your father is one of them, of course, but he's had to play a cautious role. I thought Ramachundra was another, but recent information makes me doubt it. Fred, when you come right down to it, your guess is as good as mine. Probably the new ship is being sent here on some kind of a test, and something about the trip is supposed to help us. I frankly don't see how it can matter, in the long run. I doubt that your father has any idea how close to failure we are."

"Yeah." Fred was thinking of the ruined tractor, which helped force the colony that much closer to failure. He didn't bring it up, nor did Gantry seem to be thinking of it.

The next day, the radio news reported that officers in the Ground Command section had been quizzed by the House committee investigating Station affairs. Following that, the head of the investigation released a resolution to the press demanding that the *Cosmic Egg* be taken out of the jurisdiction of the Space Agency and put back under the older Joint Military Command, on the theory that the *Egg* must not be restricted to flights between Earth and the Station. It was obviously a ruse, since no one had suggested the ship was to be used only for that. Colonel Halpern was asked to come to Earth immediately in order to testify before the investigating committee.

Late at night another news flash came over. Colonel Halpern had refused to testify that week on the basis that technical difficulties at the Station required his presence. It was a refusal which seemed to convey no defiance of the committee, but they took it as such.

Fred was fairly certain that his father had meant to defy them, and that any technical difficulties must have been created deliberately as an excuse. It was dangerous politics, he was sure; he knew that in the long run a committee could not be kept from making any investigation it chose. His father must be stalling for time; that indicated a desperation hard to accept.

Yet he didn't worry about it too much. He'd developed an enormous faith in his father's ability to judge accurately any situation not concerned with family affairs.

The work on the tractors was proceeding faster than Fred had thought possible. For one thing, Poorhouse and Boland proved to be a team who could work together reassembling the undercarriages as if they had trained for years at it. Fred was able to help, although he had to admit they were doing most of the work. They seemed to have an instinct which put both pairs of hands to work as if directed by a common brain.

On the evening of the twentieth day—the expedition had fallen into the habit of dating everything from the time they first left Emmett Base—Dr. Sessions announced that the work was finished. Although much of the repair work was makeshift, he was satisfied that the tractors were in better condition than they had been before the first trip. Almost three weeks had been lost from the original schedule, but some of the loss might be made up. Everyone was now more adjusted to life here, and Sessions hoped there would be less difficulty from bad habits once they reached the exploration site.

They could have pulled out at once, but he picked

the middle of the next day—or twenty-four hour period—for departure. By then the sun would be rising in the east, making long, harsh shadows that were a nuisance, but the light would cause the least trouble when it was behind them. Their pace should bring them to the cache and the untried mountain range with the light still at their rear. Such light should be helpful in spotting a possible route over the range.

Fred realized this would require their making about the same speed going back as had been possible on the return to Base. The tractors and trailers now were heavily loaded with supplies. The cab of his tractor was filled until there was hardly room for two men besides himself. It would be rough going, but Sessions must have considered that.

Sessions pulled something out of an envelope and spread it out. "One more thing," he said. "I've got a resolution here, signed by twenty of you. I suppose it has to be taken care of. Mr. Halpern, this concerns you, so I suggest you read it before we dispose of the matter."

Fred glanced at it, shock running through him. It was a petition to Dr. Sessions asking to have Fred Halpern replaced as a tractor driver and left behind with the other pilots. There were a lot of reasons—according to the first, he hadn't signed on as a regular member, but as a pilot. But the final one was the key. It was the belief of those signing that the number of accidents and difficulties in which he had been involved, though not clearly his responsibility, proved that he was a potential danger to the entire expedition.

It was signed, as Dr. Sessions had said, by twenty out of the twenty-seven other members of the expedition.

CHAPTER 11 /

Signs of Life

THERE WERE angry expressions on a number of faces as Fred handed the paper back to the leader. Obviously they hadn't intended the petition to be read by the man against whom it was drawn. Sessions took it and ripped it slowly to shreds.

"I don't run this expedition by petition," he said. "You were all signed on with the clear understanding that I was to lead. I intend to. There has to be one man responsible in a business like this, and he has to have sole responsibility. If anyone wishes to withdraw now, he may do so. Otherwise, you'll accept my decisions with no further attempts to change them. Well?"

There were no offers to quit. He had expected none.

"All right then, the petition is rejected." He relaxed a little. "I appreciate the fact that seven of you didn't sign this nasty little document, though. Fred, you'll take the lead tractor, as usual. We leave at noon, Earth Greenwich time, so I'd like to go over the route with you, if you'll come with me."

It was the only way to relieve a bad situation; Fred was glad to follow him to the cab of the tractor. However they had already been over the route thoroughly.

"Maybe you should have dropped me, sir," he suggested as they sat down. He couldn't blame the signers, though it hurt.

Sessions shook his head firmly. "Absolutely not. If I

gave in on this, there wouldn't be a thing done from now on without arguments, petitions, and haggling—no group like this can work that way. Besides, I happen to think you've been doing a good job, and I'll stick by you. I told your father you were one of the best men I had, and I meant it. I still mean it."

Fred tried to thank him, but he couldn't find words. Sessions brushed it aside and stood up. "They'll need a chance to gripe and grumble, so wait a while before you go back. You won't have any trouble then. I'm going to see Governor Gantry."

He was right, Fred found. When the boy slipped into the bunkroom, there were a few sullen looks and some awkwardness, but nobody said anything. Boland clapped him on the back as he went by. "Better turn in, kid. You've got a hard day ahead."

It was a hard day, though not because of the driving. It was difficult to avoid thinking of those who resented him or acting overly grateful to the ones who hadn't signed the petition. The work of driving the tractor helped. The change in light took up most of his attention at first. The sun was barely above the horizon, distorting everything.

Every rock seemed like a long projection as its dense shadow stretched away from it. Every crack in the surface appeared to be a black pit. It was something like the effect of the headlights, yet worse because the whole surface was lit. Nevertheless, it was far better than driving into the setting sun. In time, as they got accustomed to them, the effects of light and shadow began to become clearer.

They were moving westward at almost the same speed as the terminator—the sharp line between night and day. There was no true dawn or twilight, since there was no air to diffuse light, so the separation was nearly as sharp between light and dark as if it had been printed. This meant they would make most of the trip under the same conditions. It would give them all the practice they needed before crossing the chain of mountains beyond the cache.

The tractors were behaving perfectly, and they were making good time. Dr. Sessions was planning to keep moving, using relief drivers, and there seemed no mechanical reason for questioning the safety of his decision. The men would arrive at the final destination a little more tired, a small price to pay for the time saved.

Through the first day it seemed to Fred that everyone was watching him, as if to see what his reaction to the petition might be. He did his best to show nothing, aware that anything which might split the group into quarreling factions must be avoided. After the final stop for dinner, there seemed to be a gradual relaxing. Nothing was said, but most of the men began treating him as they had done before the trouble. Perhaps they even seemed more friendly. Talk was close to normal in the dormitory trailer before he went to sleep.

This time the pass through the mountains—the pass used on the trip back to Base—was familiar to them. They hardly had to slacken speed as they drove on. The only change was the need to turn on their headlights after the first few miles, when the cliffs cut off the sun. Light glared against the rocks far above them and was reflected down, but it was too unreliable for driving. Even after they were through the peaks, for many miles the shadow of the mountains left them in a world of darkness.

This time they could follow their own trail through the plains. The dust tended to settle back under its own weight, but the passage of the vehicles had left enough traces for a sharp eye. Having proved safe once, the trail could be followed at full speed.

They reached the cache on the twenty-fifth day "after Base." Here they stopped to readjust some of the load. Fred's tractor remained a little cramped with extra oxygen bottles, food, water and other necessities, while half of the load was transferred to the small trailers.

These were hitched onto the tractors, as was the laboratory headquarters.

They set out again with full supplies. They were better stocked now than they would have been had no trouble arisen. The amount they brought on this trip was more than had been used before; to that extent, the expedition was better off.

The mountains, which had looked impenetrable in the darkness, were now broken by chasms and gorges that offered some hope of a trail through them. Sessions studied them against his map. Finally he selected what seemed to be the best way through. If no pass could be found, the tractors would have to make a detour of more than two hundred miles around the end of the mountain chain.

The dawn light aided them at first. The sun was shining directly into the openings through the first ranges, and they could see most of the obstacles well in advance. It might prove more difficult once they were well into the ugly peaks, but they could turn back in the light if there was no way through.

Within a few miles, they began to run into areas where the light was poor, or where picking a trail was a matter of difficult decision. Sessions sent men ahead when possible to survey the route. Once a man got a few hundred feet higher than the trail, it was often easier to find ways that could be negotiated easily. A team of two men moved more rapidly than the tractors dared, and human legs were able to climb where no tractor could.

Halfway through the mountains, things got more difficult. The center of a range always seemed rougher; toward the outer sections, the number of passages increased. The light was totally unreliable now. It glared down from the peaks, reflecting the sunlight; by the time it was reflected back and forth several times, it was too weak to help.

They came to a sharp break finally. Here the trail

dropped away into a fissure a hundred feet across and impassable even for men on ropes. On the other side the route they had followed seemed to go on, but the problem was to find a way around the fissure. The photographs were useless for discovering such a path.

Boland had been driving. Fred went to volunteer for one of the survey teams. Sessions looked doubtful, but agreed. "Better take Dr. Wallace. He's ready to go out."

There were two teams this time, each carrying a powerful battery and light. They were going to backtrack to a lower section, then follow that to what might be a road to the bottom of the fissure. There Fred and Wallace would work their way up to the trail beyond the fissure to see whether it would do, while the second team was to explore another possibility to the left, where a ledge seemed to jut out far enough to serve as a road for the tractors. The second group would be made up of Dr. Villiers, the biologist, and a small, pleasant man named Whitley.

The path branching off from the one they had followed led directly to the bottom of the fissure. Finding a way up to the continuation of the trail beyond the fissure proved to be tricky, though. Fred located a way up which they could climb but it was not adequate for the tractors. They hoped to do better hunting from above.

Their radios were permanently open, so he heard Villiers and Whitley moving along their route.

"We're twisting around down here," the biologist said. His signal was no longer coming in directly. It bounced off the rocky walls and was reflected to them. "It looks as if we'll wind up back on top with you."

Wallace motioned Fred to follow and struck out to see whether they could locate a place where the lower path climbed up to meet the one they were on. They were just rounding a turn with Wallace ahead when Fred stopped abruptly. He'd seen something in the reflection from his light and failed to recognize it at first.

Now it hit him. He called out to Wallace and went back quickly.

It took a little searching, then his light caught it at just the right angle. He yelled at what was before him.

It wasn't very impressive. Reaching to a height of not more than four or five inches, it grew out of a small crack in a rocky section. He would never have seen it except by accident. Small as it was, it could be the most important thing ever found on the Moon. It looked like a living plant.

He couldn't be sure. It was a spindly, spiny little thing, faintly green, appearing to be made of dry plastic rather than living tissue. Life on the Moon could not be like that on Earth; the water and air needed for soft growth wasn't there. It might be only a strange crystal formation; Fred had seen chemical crystals grow, almost like little mineral trees and bushes. Somehow, this growth seemed different. Its branches had a look of purpose, as if reaching for the light that came down faintly from above, and there was a cluster at the end of one branch that might be a seed or a spore sack.

He found himself trembling as he got up from his knees. If there were life here—even a single living plant-life thing—the excitement of the discovery would bring enough expeditions from Earth to keep the colony humming and active for years.

Wallace was moving forward; Fred waved him back. He wanted Dr. Villiers, who would know what to do about the plant, and whether it was a true sign of life.

He could see Villiers and Whitley moving onto the far end of the trail. Villiers was signaling with the light and talking continuously. Obviously they had found a way up here, and the tractors must be following behind. Fred tried to get a word in, but there was no free channel. The tractors should be directly below, from the way Villiers was moving close to the edge, bending so his helmet antenna stuck out just beyond the cliff.

"Dr. Villiers!" This time Fred's call penetrated, and

the biologist looked up. "Dr. Villiers, I've found something you've got to see."

Villiers gasped. He didn't have to be told to know what would call for his full attention. Fred hadn't dared to put the thought of life into words until he could be more certain. Villiers turned and touched helmets with Whitley, then came trotting forward rapidly, while the other man took up the signaling.

"Where?" the biologist asked sharply as he touched his helmet to Fred's. "And is it . . . ?"

"I don't know for sure—it looks like a plant," Fred answered. "Back here about fifteen feet . . ."

A wild yell from Wallace brought their heads up sharply. Fred felt his muscles knot savagely at what he saw.

Whitley had been moving along the edge, apparently trying to beam his signal down toward the tractors. He seemed to pay no attention as his foot moved on. He stepped on the small rock Wallace had seen, and it rolled under him.

They were all too far from Whitley to help him, and would not have dared to try; a sudden touch might startle him and make him lose his balance.

Amazingly, Whitley seemed to right himself. He gave a faint cry of surprise at the first touch of the stone. Apparently he had cut off his receiver to divert all the battery power into the transmitter and had not heard the warning cry from Wallace. There was no terror in his reactions. He took a twisting, half-dancing step as the stone moved under him, and his arms flailed out like those of a tight-rope walker. He almost recovered his balance. His step carried him a few inches back from the edge where he had been, and his next one nearly brought him to safety.

Then another fragment of rock was in his path, and there was no way to avoid it. His foot came down on it, sliding sideways. His ankle seemed to turn under him. Now, for the first time, he cried out in fear.

It was too late for help. The man's body twisted again, this time in the wrong way. His other foot skidded, and he half-leaped in an attempt to recover. The effort merely sent him upward a few inches, but could not check his outward motion. He seemed to drift over the edge of the cliff and to coast downward.

The cries of fright cut off as his helmet disappeared beyond the edge. A second later, they came again in some signal by reflection. Then there was no sound from him.

Fred felt his heart pounding and heard the rasping of his breath. His stomach churned; he managed to master it before he could be sick in his suit. Beside him, Villiers was bent over, retching. Wallace seemed frozen, like a figure carved out of stone.

"Wallace!" Fred called thickly, and got a weak answering nod. "Go below and find the tractors. Bring them here at once. I'll look for Whitley."

Wallace hesitated, then turned back along the trail, moving uncertainly. Fred approached the place where Whitley had gone over. He got down on his hands and knees, then flat on his stomach. There was no use in taking chances on some fault that would weaken the ledge, even though it seemed to have held Whitley's weight. There would be no advantage in having two men fall. He wriggled his way cautiously toward the edge and finally stuck his helmet over.

In the beam of his headlight, there wasn't much to be seen at first. On the other side of the yawning pit, he could see the trail with one of the tractors just moving out of sight. Between the ledge being used as a path and the cliff where he lay, Fred could see only a great hole that seemed to go down beyond the range of his light. It was far too deep for any man to fall the entire distance and live. Even if all allowances were made for the weaker gravity, such a drop had to be fatal.

He swept his light up the nearer edge, looking for anything that might have caught the body. Shock must have numbed his senses at first, because he suddenly became aware that he was looking for a tree or vine such as might grow from a cliff on Earth. There could be none here.

There was a ledge perhaps fifty feet down, where the cliff curved back below Fred. It ended in a sort of pocket, like a groove cut in the rock. This was strewn with boulders, and pitted as if gas bubbles had broken, marring the smoothness of the stone.

He swept his light across it, but there was no sign of a spacesuited body.

He was shifting position when Villiers' quaking voice reached him. The man had managed to get control of himself. Now he was on the edge, looking over as was Fred. "See if we can cross our headlights, get rid of some of the shadows."

He was far enough away to make it worth while, but there were no results. They could not see anything that resembled Whitley among the rock fragments on the ledge.

Fred moved farther forward, to make sure his antenna was well over the edge so a signal would reach all parts of the ledge.

"Whitley!" he called. He kept calling, shifting to one after another of the five frequencies the set handled. But there was no sound from below.

If Whitley had gone all the way down, there would be no response. The radio should be as dead as the man.

CHAPTER 12 /

Trouble Trail

THE EXPEDITION reached the top of the ledge a few minutes later, the tractors laboring up at low speed. They headed away from Fred and stopped. The trailers began disgorging people. Someone took Villiers and led him off to clean up. The rest spread out, well back from the edge of the cliff. This time, nobody had to tell them to keep out of the way.

Dr. Sessions and Boland brought a light powerful enough to reach the distant bottom, but Fred didn't watch. He was back where he'd first seen Whitley fall, trying to remember everything. Anything falling in a vacuum obeys the laws of some kind of an orbit or trajectory; with knowledge of his speed and the pull of gravity, Whitley's fall could be predicted.

It was hard, trying to reconstruct the flight from the little he had seen, instead of sensing it directly; at the time, horror had paralyzed the strange sense in his head. Or maybe it had worked, but the message had never become conscious.

He was reasonably sure when he joined the group, however. "Dr. Sessions, he didn't reach bottom. The way he was falling, he would have struck against that ledge just below us, and he'd have landed far enough inside it not to be thrown out again. He must be there, even if we can't see him from here. I'd like to be let down on a rope to see."

There were doubtful looks from some of the men. Sessions didn't look scornful, but he wasn't convinced. He'd put the computing incident into the background and dismissed it, never fully believing it.

Someone began explaining why Whitley couldn't have landed on the ledge, making the mathematics sound completely convincing. He'd have been right, if the cliff curved at exactly the angle he believed, but it didn't fit the path of the body Fred had seen. Sessions cut off the argument abruptly and seemed to consider the idea.

Finally he shrugged. "You'll be taking a chance— something down there might rip your suit or cut the line. And I'm not sold on your estimate, Fred. If you're at all right, however, we can't afford not to try it. Have you figured out how to work it?"

Boland came forward with a better plan than Fred's rough one, and they nodded as he finished. The biggest problem was getting a rope over the edge without letting it wear against the rock. But they had enough material to rig up a crude hoist that would carry the weight of two men. At Sessions' nod of approval, Boland chose men to help him and to get the parts. Fred replaced his oxygen and gave all his equipment a final check. The little structure of rods and spare parts, braced and weighted down by six volunteers, was already hanging over the edge when he returned.

The worst part was the first step. Fred sat in the loop of rope at the edge, then he was eased out carefully, to avoid putting a strain on the device. It was a long way down, and his eyes couldn't avoid the ugly blackness below, where the lights failed to pierce. He felt the hoist start to lower him, and brought his attention back to the work.

Either by accident or good planning on Boland's part, the rope eased him down to a bare spot on the ledge. It was deeper, he saw, than it had appeared from above. There was no sign of a body.

He slipped from the rope and began exploring, moving with as much care as he could. Rocks were piled up one on top of another in a disorder that threatened to break free and roll over the edge at the first disturbance. He made his way around one pile, found nothing, and went on.

Behind the second pile, he found Whitley. The man must have struck and been thrown back and sideways. There was no sign of movement, and the helmet was cracked, while the radio was broken and useless. The damage hadn't rendered the suit airless—its swelling showed there was still pressure. Then, as Fred watched, there was the faintest movement of his chest. He was alive.

Fred moved him as little as possible while checking for air leaks. There might be tiny ones; they wouldn't matter in the few minutes more it would take. Finally, he lifted Whitley, hoping there were no broken vertebrae to worry about; an injured spine could kill him during the rescue. The risk had to be taken.

As he picked up the man, a faint sound came through from suit to suit. Fred bent to press his helmet to Whitley's and spoke quickly. "It's all right, Whitley. We'll have you topside in a couple more minutes."

"Darned fool," the other's voice said softly. "Didn't look where I was going. Nuisance. Thanks."

Fred wasn't wasting time trying to call those above him. He carried Whitley back carefully. It was an effort to get into the sling and take him in his arms again, but he made it. The rope began lifting at the first signal. Several minutes later, men were taking foolish chances near the edge as they eased Whitley away from Fred, then pulled Fred in where he could slip out of the loop.

Boland waved Fred back to the trailer as he began breaking up the improvised rig. But Fred was looking for Villiers.

The biologist was obviously torn between a feeling that Fred needed a rest and his own eagerness. Now that the rescue had been made, they both suddenly remembered the plant Fred thought he had seen.

Fred took the older man's arm and began to lead him off, waving back a couple of worried people who seemed to think he needed rest. He touched the biologist's helmet. "I don't want anyone to know until you confirm what I think it is," he said. There was no use raising false hopes that might be dashed, on top of all the other strains they'd just been through. His legs were still feeling a reaction from everything.

He paused, studying the stone around them. "It was about here . . ."

Then he spotted the rock. The place was right, the little fissure in it was as he remembered it. But there was no plantlike thing.

Villiers gasped as he saw Fred's face change. They both moved forward. There were footprints all over here, and the marks of hobnails from someone's boot were ground faintly into the very rock where the plant had been. There was no evidence of anything which could ever have lived.

Fred tried to describe it as it had been, while Villiers studied the ground and the rock. If there had been anything like roots, they were gone. At last he stood up, looking like a man promised immortality, only to have it snatched away.

"I don't know, Fred. I can't tell, from what you say. It wouldn't matter—any life existing here would have to be almost crystalline in dryness, I suspect. It would shatter like a true crystal if anyone touched it." Then his face lightened a little. "Well, it's something to hope on. If there was one, maybe there are more someplace. You've given me a little more evidence than those rumors in the colony, at least. All right, we'd better go back before someone gets suspicious."

Then he glanced at the edge of the cliff and back to the place where the plant had been. "There may be more plants, but there couldn't be another Ted Whitley. I guess we're lucky."

In a few hours, the expedition reached the top of the divide through the mountains and began heading down. Fred had taken over the driving again, in spite of protests. He felt as capable as he could hope to feel, and the work might do him good. Boland stayed for a while, and then nodded, as if satisfied everything was going well.

"Whitley's pretty badly bruised, and he's got a sprained ankle. But he'll be all right in a couple more days. I hear he's issued an ultimatum to our friend Mona Williams—the next time she opens her mouth about you, he's threatened to pull her tongue out. I've got a feeling most of the rest of us feel the same, kid. Well, take it easy."

He climbed out to return to the trailer for a rest. Fred went on driving, cautiously easing down the cluttered, winding trail. There were times when men had to go out to scout the way, but the pass proved far less difficult than they had expected. For once, the photographs seemed to have shown all the major details.

By the time his shift was over, they were moving down steadily onto another flat plain. It was one of the places where the basic level was badly broken by small outcroppings and numerous tiny craters. Driving required constant attention, at least until they could get beyond the dark shadows of the mountains. The long trip was coming to an end.

It wasn't entirely over, however. One of the trailers found a hole in the ground exactly the size needed to make it drop violently down on one side. There was a snapping sound inside, and when they pulled it out they found an axle had been broken off cleanly. It was something no one had expected. With many wheels on each side to hold the trailer up, no single wheel should have received such a jolt.

They were out of the shadow by then, and they

stopped to eat and survey the damage. Boland and Fred managed to get far enough under the trailer to free the whole axle and work it out. The only thing they could do was to weld it. There was some doubt as to whether their welding torch was powerful enough to handle the job.

Fred began the work. He'd done some welding at the Station, and he'd had a course in repairing motors which included the use of such equipment. They were using an oxyacetylene torch, since it required less weight than any equivalent electrical installation.

"At least we don't have to worry much about corrosion here," Boland said as he watched the blue flame through his helmet shield. "Nothing like having a vacuum around you at a time like this."

Fred was about to agree when he noticed something that made no sense. The metal had been completely bright when he laid it down. Now there was a faint film around one spot. He reached out to wipe it off, but it wasn't dust. He began scanning the ground.

Then he saw a faint stirring in the fine dust. In one small spot, it seemed to lift up slightly. Boland grunted and shoveled the dust aside, to get down to the ground half an inch below. When they looked closely there was a tiny hole.

Sessions came over at their call and studied it. "Gas escaping, all right. It must have been trapped down there until a tractor passed over it and cracked that little hole. We've seen evidence of such gas before, but never traced it down. Get a bottle and collect some of it."

Erica Neufeld brought the bottles—little plastic balloonlike flasks. She was a chemist as well as a geologist, and her small face was beaming as one of the flasks slowly filled. "Wonderful. Absolutely wonderful. What marvelous luck that axle broke right here!"

"Hardly what I'd call luck," Boland commented, but he was smiling.

She was staring at the flask. "It is, though. We may learn more about the nature of the crust from this than anything else. When I can get a few of these filled and start analyzing the gas, we'll have a key to all kinds of activity down there. There must be sulfur in it—that's what caused the corrosion on that alloy you were welding—and some trace of water vapor. Sulfur won't act like that without water and . . ."

Fred and Boland left her to her specimens and moved the axle to another spot where there would be no further trouble. Here the welding went according to plan. But Fred was thinking that Villiers should have one of the specimens of the gas, or a report on it. He'd want to know about any possible organic compounds. Also, if there were water vapor and perhaps oxygen, such seepage might account for the possibility of life.

When they finished with the axle, it seemed as good as new. Anyhow, in normal use there would be no great strain at the welded spot. They found that Erica had finally collected all the gas she could use and that Dr. Villiers hadn't needed a suggestion from Fred to take his own samplings. By the time the trailer was ready to move, the whole expedition was speculating on the work already being done in the laboratory.

For a time, things went smoothly. But it seemed that on the Moon nothing could work properly for any length of time. Again, it was Fred's tractor where the trouble started. He found that he was shoving up the power higher and higher to get the same response out of the motor. At lunch, he checked his supply of peroxide fuel and whistled unhappily when he saw how much had been used. There must be a leak somewhere that was robbing him of efficiency.

There was no way of finding it from a quick check, though he crawled under the carriage while Boland ran the motor through its speeds with the clutches disengaged.

Sessions chuckled bitterly. "You're obviously a jinx,

Fred," he said. There was no animosity in the remark, and Fred realized that the leader wouldn't have made it if anyone would take it seriously. That resentment of him had mysteriously vanished since he'd been right about where Whitley had landed. Except for Mona Williams, he now had the feeling that the whole expedition was friendly.

"I stick pins in little models of the tractor," he retorted. "It's pure black magic. But I think we can go on until night. I've got sort of a plan to find the leak then, if I can find the right spot."

"Okay, Fred. If you see what you want, signal us to stop and we'll make a full night's delay of it. I've been thinking of going back to single shift, anyhow, to let us reach the main site rested and ready to work."

It was an hour after the usual time for dinner when Fred located a dust pit that looked promising. He prodded the edges with a welding rod and decided it would be deep enough. Then he outlined his idea to Boland.

After dinner, they unhitched the tractor and backed it toward the dust trap.

"Did you really need one that big?" the geologist asked.

The flat surface stretched out for nearly two miles, indicating that the depression must be a huge one. Fred shook his head. It was the first he had found that seemed large enough.

They arranged signals. One man had to be inside the tractor, and one outside. That meant using a system of banging on the tractor to signal what the driver was to do. Finally, satisfied, Fred went out. He was smaller and lighter, better equipped to trace the motor, and generally the obvious man for the outside work.

At his signal, Boland backed the tractor slowly into the dust. There was a smooth slope leading into the depth of the pit, and the tractor sank slowly as it backed. When it reached a level where the motor just touched the dust, Fred signaled for a halt, and began crawling under it.

The idea was simple. Any leak would stir the dust, then he could trace it to the source. It wouldn't have to be a large opening; a hole too small to be seen easily could account for all the waste. It was like sticking an inner tube into water to find where the hole was by tracing the bubbles.

Slowly, a step at a time, the tractor was backed further and further out, until the motor was nearly covered. Fred's job was getting harder. He had to push his way through the dust and then get his head up to study the action of the surface under his headlight. Soon there would be no room for him to see. Even a little way below the surface, there was no visibility at all, for the light couldn't penetrate the dust.

Then he grunted in satisfaction. The dust was swirling faintly around one section of the pipe that led from the throttle to the injector. He piled up enough dust in his hands to pinpoint the trouble and marked it off with a soft red crayon. The wax of the crayon melted against the warm pipe, and a tiny bubble arose on the surface. It would have taken hours of work to locate the place any other way; now the little pit in the wax could be found at any time. The pipe would not get hot enough to melt it all off.

He crawled out painfully and stood up to bang on the tractor as a signal that it was completed. Boland was ready. The treads spun, working hard against the dust. Great clouds were thrown up from the spinning belts of silicone rubber, and the tractor began moving out.

Fred stepped back to avoid the dust, brushing it off his helmet. He took another step, and another . . .

The bottom dropped out from under him, and he went down slowly until his helmet was completely covered. The dust yielded beneath him another few feet until he touched bottom.

Grumbling, he twisted around to feel the edges of the

hole into which he'd dropped. He'd been foolish to move where he hadn't tested. Once he found the upward slope again, it wouldn't matter.

Fifteen minutes later, he was completely lost in the lightless, almost liquid stuff that surrounded him.

CHAPTER 13 /

SOS from Space

FRED STOPPED, realizing he'd made the worst possible mistake; he'd been acting, not thinking. Now he had no clear idea of how deep he was in the dust or in what direction an exit lay. He couldn't even be sure that he wasn't going in a circle. Backtracking was as impossible as moving forward.

Since he couldn't be sure of finding his way out, the only solution was to stay put and let others find him. It was harder to stand still while his oxygen bubbled away slowly, but a lot more intelligent. All he could do was to help them locate him.

That presented a problem. He was sure he was too deep to create any motion on the surface, unless he opened his oxygen supply to full delivery and hoped someone could see the dust bubbles from that. However it was only a desperation measure. There had to be some better way. He assumed someone must be watching the surface for any sign, if he could give it.

Then he relaxed. He had the rod he had first used to estimate the depth of the dust for the tractor. It was large enough to be seen, and it could be tossed fairly accurately toward the surface, even through the slight resistance of the dust.

He balanced it on his glove, estimating the throw. The dust couldn't be more than twenty feet above his head—there'd been no noticeable feeling that he was heading downward. The rod had to clear the surface, but not rise too high, or it would travel too great a distance and be hard to locate again. It also had to go at a slight angle, since he had no desire to have it strike him on the return at the risk of puncturing a hole in his helmet or stunning him. He plotted the trajectory in his head until it felt right, then tossed the rod upward.

A few seconds later, there was a faint but sharp metallic sound transmitted from the ground through his boots. He moved cautiously forward, feeling about with his feet. In five steps, he felt the rod. This time he turned about face before throwing it. Again there was the sound of the rod striking.

This time it was followed by another sound. There was a double tap.

He located the rod and banged it sharply against the ground below him, twice this time. There was an answering tapping. The third time, the tapping seemed nearer, and the fourth time there was no question; someone was heading toward the sound he had made.

Suddenly something brushed against his chest, and his fingers identified it as a rope. He pulled it to him sharply. Now he could hear footsteps coming from the ground through his suit. There was almost no time lapse before a hand groped against him and caught his shoulder. A helmet was pressed against his, and Ted Whitley's voice said, "Turnabout's fair play, Fred. Grab the rope and come on!"

The rope twitched several times, apparently in a signal. Then it grew taut as it was pulled forward. Fred let it guide him.

In less than five minutes, his helmet broke through the dust surface, and he could see his rescuers. The rope seemed to have been pieced together out of everything available, and most of the expedition were somewhere along it in the dust. One end reached a spot beside the tractor where Dr. Sessions held it to guide them all back. He held a hand to his antenna as Fred looked and then pointed. Fred turned to see Whitley, who still walked with a slight limp. He was carrying a pole of some sort on which an antenna had been strapped, high enough to stay above the dust.

"Thought you'd know we'd come after you," the man said. "Good thing, or we might have had to spend another fifteen minutes before we could be sure of surrounding you and circling in. How do you feel?"

Fred took a deeper breath as his feet finally came free of the dust. "Grateful," he said. "Foolish. And dusty."

He knew there'd be cracks and jokes at his expense for the next day or so, but he also knew he wouldn't mind. He was feeling better than he had any right to. He let them lead him into the dining dormitory and dutifully drank the coffee they insisted on forcing on him while he tried to explain why he'd gotten into the trouble and how it had felt. He half expected a dressing down from Dr. Sessions, but the leader only grinned.

"We'll all do something foolish before this is over," Sessions said. "Let's hope we can keep our heads when it happens and avoid any serious consequences. How about that motor?"

It gave Fred the opening he'd been seeking, and in another few minutes he went out with Boland and tackled the job. Now that they knew where to make the weld, the work was routine. It didn't look pretty when he finished, but it should hold; he'd been careful to make sure there were no impurities in the weld which would trigger a peroxide breakdown before the fuel reached the motor. Everything tested out afterward; the next day the tractor was operating at full efficiency.

On the twenty-seventh day and without further trouble, they reached the site Sessions had chosen and began making a permanent camp. The trailers would still serve as their living quarters, but there was a lot of work getting everything in order and redistributing supplies. The tractors would be used mostly for scouting and detail work; each had to carry a portable plastic tent, extra supplies of oxygen and food, and all the fuel it could store. There would be times when a driver might have numerous trips from place to place without time to return to the main camp.

The camp itself was against a tiny cliff that rose from a small outcropping of rock. It was slightly higher than most of the surrounding territory, serving as a lookout post for Sessions to keep track of much of the movement that would go on throughout the area.

Fred was never very clear about much of the work. He understood a little. Teams were assigned to make borings through the crust, then the cores raised by the boring bits—hollow bits holding whatever they cut out until it was removed—were classified and studied. There was a system for the location of these borings, but the theory behind it was far beyond his grasp.

Other teams were sent out on a rigid schedule to plant small explosive charges in holes in the ground. These had to be set off at the exact second called for. There were other teams with delicate instruments which measured the shock transmitted through the ground. Finally, at the top of the cliff and as far from the camp as possible, the main seismograph was installed carefully, and connected directly to a complicated computer in the laboratory.

He picked up a little from the talk. Even the speed of sound through the crust was important, it seemed, as well as the shape of the shock wave. Here many of the minerals were quite different from those on Earth. The elements were the same, of course, but the way they formed compounds differed greatly. On Earth, the rocks were formed in an oxygen atmosphere, or at least under conditions where oxygen and even hydrogen were common, and where water was the great solvent. That accounted for many of the oxides, hydrates and hydroxides, as well as for part of the carbonates and other general minerals. Here, there was no sure way of knowing what might be found. Preliminary tests indicated that there was less difference than had been expected. There were carbonates—compounds of elements with carbon and oxygen together; the carbides, or compounds of elements with only carbon, were much more rare than had been expected. More precision was needed to make the findings meaningful.

After the very first day one thing seemed certain. The idea that all the heavy elements should be at the core of the Moon was wrong; if anything, there was a larger percentage of the total amount of heavy elements on the surface here than there was on Earth.

"The tides produced by Earth on this world must have stirred things up more than we expected," Boland told Fred. "That means we may find more stuff near the surface of Earth than we expected, too. But one thing is sure—there is going to be more than enough mineral resources here for a colony. It may take us time to locate it, but we've already decided that there must be uranium. We're sending out a pair with radiation detectors to investigate."

And now, for the first time, Fred and the others saw the real Mona Williams. She was no more pleasant than before, but she was an absolute genius at getting meaningful results from what seemed like insignificant data out of the computing machines. She was responsible for at least half of the programs on which they began to work, some of which had never been dreamed of before the expedition left Earth.

Fred began to suspect that her resentment of him went back further than he had thought. It must have dated from their first meeting when she heard his claim that he could plot a course in his head. To her, obviously, the highest order of merit in the universe was the computer. She could never believe that any human being could do what a machine was designed for. She might even have been jealous of him, as a computer would have felt jealousy if it had feelings.

Although he couldn't like her, he found himself respecting her. She might love machines more than men, but her work would help the colonists as much as that of anyone else.

The teams were just beginning to loosen up and find directions for their work on the thirtieth day when a brief announcement reached them on high-powered radio beam from the Station. It was a rebroadcast of the regular Earth news, and it hit them all when played back from the tape.

The *Cosmic Egg* had been launched from the Station on a supposed test flight to the Moon. On board were Major Wickman as pilot and Dr. Ramachundra as observer. The Committee on Space was investigating the flight, which had apparently been authorized by Colonel Halpern aboard the Station only two hours before an official order canceling all tests pending further investigation.

"Your father's in hot water now," Sessions told Fred. "Boiling hot! But he beat them. Now let's hope it was worth it."

Fred had no words to describe his feelings. He was torn between worry and admiration, doubt and fear for his father. Colonel Halpern must have had a means of leaking information out of the committee, just as they had leaks from the Station. Whatever the reason, he'd obviously decided that the trip was worth any risk to himself. Now with the ship beyond all national limits in space, nobody could issue any meaningful orders to Wickman until he reached the Moon—then the orders would come from Gantry.

He remembered Gantry's doubts about the helpfulness of Ramachundra, and again began to worry. He knew his father would never regret the action, no matter what happened to him, if it furthered man's career in space. But if there had been some mistake about the representative from the World Congress, it would be a pretty horrible thing.

There wasn't anything anyone could do, however. The *Cosmic Egg* would attain a higher speed than the ships of the expedition and would land in three days. They would have to wait until then.

A later news broadcast took off some of the pressure. When the chips were down, Colonel Halpern had at least as many friends in Congress and in the Administration as he had enemies, and as important ones. The committee wasn't going to get him removed from his position without a long and complicated fight. By the time that was finished, the whole issue might be decided by what happened on the Moon.

There wasn't too much time for worry, though. Fred was kept on a steady round of trips. Sessions was using his tractor as a means of keeping all efforts coördinated. The machine was on constant duty to carry the leader from project to project or to rush some suddenly needed equipment from point to point.

The first crude picture of the crust was beginning to take shape. Fred saw some of the graphs, and there were parts that could be understood by a layman. There seemed to be great pockets of emptiness under the surface, and other bubbles which might hold liquids— probably water, since oil seemed impossible without the presence of highly active life. There were other sections that indicated the possibility of valuable deposits of heavy metals. So far, they had not found out very much about uranium deposits. The radiation detectors reported a fairly large field in one place, but its richness and depth were still subject to doubt.

The one area of research where no progress had been made was in the hunt for life. Dr. Villiers made elaborate tests of the cores brought up by the boring bits, looking for compounds which might prove that there had ever been life here. The evidence was doubtful. A few compounds were technically organic, but there was reason to believe such material might be created without the presence of life on this airless world.

He spent most of his free time riding about with Fred, looking for some hint of a living thing. He'd done an elaborate job of analyzing the conditions around the rock where Fred saw the plantlike growth and even investigated the rumors of life reported by the colonists. But none of his work was paying off.

"Maybe there is no life in this whole section," he mourned. "Maybe this is the dead part of the Moon. And over there, a hundred miles beyond our explorations, there may be living things any man could find at once. How can I know?"

"What about the crater where they thought they saw evidence of life in the telescopes years ago?" Fred asked him.

The scientist shrugged. "Telescopes! An earlier expedition looked into that. That crater was covered with a few bits of unstable compound. When it got hot, it took one form and showed color; when it cooled off, it went back to being colorless. Just chemical, and not much chemical at that."

There was no further news from the Station that could be picked up by the receiver in the laboratory. But everyone knew the approximate landing time for the ship. Sessions listened to the mounting excitement from the men and finally decided to call a halt to the work when the landing should be due. He was as interested as anyone else. Except for a few people who had to stay at their posts for some experiment, the whole group was in the laboratory when the thirty-third day came. The news had become more important than anything else to them.

Nothing was being broadcast by the Station on the news frequencies. Mona Williams switched over to the channel reserved for the ships. There was still nothing. Probably by the time the ship began landing checks it would be far below their horizon, where no signals could reach them.

Fred felt the tension building up tightly in himself.

He spotted one of the pairs of binoculars on the desk near him, grabbed them up and began fastening his helmet.

"Put it on the helmet receivers," he called as he headed for the air lock. It could be rebroadcast if anything came through, and he would miss nothing by being outside.

The binoculars had been designed for use from a helmet; nevertheless he expected to find nothing except by accident. The landing jets would be small streaks in the immense area of the sky. He found a place behind a trailer where the shadow gave him better seeing and began searching. Someone was beside him. Sessions, he guessed, but kept sweeping the skies overhead.

Abruptly sound broke from his helmet phones. It was a harsh clicking of Morse code, followed by coördinate signals, all being transmitted by the automatic sender in the ship.

It was the ancient distress signal. "SOS! SOS! . . ."

Fred caught the coördinates and jerked the binoculars up. Then he groaned. The *Cosmic Egg* had four great rockets arranged together in the tail; all should have been blasting out. Even at the distance that separated them, Fred could see that there were only two streaks instead of the great wash of flame the four should have made together. Something must have ruined half of the motors of the ship.

Now he could see other tiny pinpoints of flame above the main jets. The *Egg* had side rockets instead of gyros for steering, and they were being used too. The main jets seemed to twinkle, first slowly, then with a rising frequency that turned the two jets into a single pattern.

Wickman was spinning the ship on its axis. It would be rotating like a top by the time he landed. Fred heard himself groaning as he realized the desperate chance the pilot was taking and guessed the reason.

Suddenly the main flame grew brighter, confirming Fred's guess. One of the motors must have failed, and the pilot had been forced to cut off the opposite one to prevent an unbalanced thrust that would drive the ship at an angle. By spinning it, he could hope the unbalance would be equalized as the rotation carried the off-center force rapidly around the center of the ship. The ship would oscillate a little, but its drive should remain steadily pointed down against the pulling force of gravity.

It meant that Wickman would be spinning about inside the control cabin with the ship, totally unable to get a stable fix on the ground below. It was something to be tried only in the hopeless last efforts of a man who knew he could never avoid a crash.

The streak of flame dropped nearer and nearer the horizon. Then the bright spot vanished, and the radio signals went dead.

CHAPTER 14/

Mutiny

BESIDE HIM, Fred heard a shuddering sigh that was probably an echo of his own. He turned to see Dr. Sessions staring through a pair of binoculars at the place where the ship had vanished. Now the scientist dropped his arms reluctantly. They turned back to the laboratory. If there was any further news, it would have to come from the Station.

Fred was drained of emotion. He was beginning to realize what Wickman must have been going through. He was a superlative pilot to have managed what he did; such a landing was something no human being had ever considered before.

Fred tried to sum it up for the others who were waiting inside the trailer. Sessions must have guessed the meaning of what he had seen, but had been unwilling to believe it. Now the leader's face grew even grimmer.

"Is there any chance they could have landed and lived?" he asked.

It was the question that was bothering Fred. He shook his head. "I don't know. If Wickman could find a place in spite of the spin, if he could keep the ship upright . . . I don't know."

The seats inside the ship would cushion a twelve gravity deceleration. The ship itself would buckle, giving around the tank section first and collapsing downward to soak up some of the shock. How high a final landing speed could it take, even if everything went perfectly? At most, five hundred miles an hour was the limit; that was only a tiny part of the velocity Wickman had to cancel with his underpowered blast.

Fred had caught the flow of coördinates, integrating them in his head with the path he had seen the ship taking. He hadn't been aware at the time, but his brain had plotted the course and probable speed of landing. There were too many variables. It came out right at the thin edge between a faint chance and certain disaster.

Mona had been running through the frequencies, listening for any message. Now she found one, and tuned it in. It was coming from the Station, apparently on a tight beam to the colony, since they could barely hear it through the solar static. At first it was only a slow speed replay from tapes of the coördinates the emergency sender had broadcast. Fred groaned as he listened to the final ones picked up after the ship had passed beyond the horizon from the expedition.

The coördinates were wrong. The spinning must have upset some delicate mechanism in the detectors and sensors that automatically located the ship in space against certain fixed stars.

Then a man's voice came on. "We've searched the entire area with the tightest angle of reception we can adjust. There's no response from the ship. Nothing is coming through, Governor Gantry. Absolutely nothing. Either the men are dead or the crash destroyed their transmitters."

There was a long pause, while Gantry answered from Emmett Base. The receiver here had no chance of picking up that side of the conversation. Then the message resumed from the Station:

"We're checking the landing course, Governor. There are some discrepancies. Something seemed to throw the plotters off there at the end, according to our computations. Better put—which one? Better put Poorhouse on and let us get what we can from his observation."

It would be Poorhouse, Fred thought bitterly. He was the one pilot with the least sense of an orbit, the one least capable of getting an idea of the course from observation. But it was lucky anyone at Base had seen the landing.

There were a series of questions then that made no sense at all without the other side of the conversation. They were probably checking their figures with Poorhouse, trying to make sense of the final course of the *Cosmic Egg*. The radio went dead.

"This is going to be tough on your father," Erica Neufeld said softly, touching Fred's arm. "I'm sorry."

Fred had considered what the wrecking of the *Cosmic Egg* would mean to Colonel Halpern, but he was helpless to do anything about it—as helpless as he seemed in all other ways.

The radio came to life again, this time listing the lunar longitude and latitude of the crash area calculated on the basis of all the data the Station could get. "We estimate the probable error as not more than plus or minus fifteen miles. You'll have to search quite a circle, Governor Gantry. I'm afraid both of your tractors will be needed for the search."

Fred sprang to the lunar map and began checking the area, though he already was sure of what he would find. He circled the spot, and his face must have looked as shocked as he felt.

"What's the matter?" Dr. Sessions asked him quickly.

"They've got the ship in the wrong place. They're over a hundred miles off, not just ten or twenty. It's so far north of where they put it that they'll never find it, no matter how hard Gantry searches."

"They can't be that far off," Sessions protested. "They've got the best brains and most advanced computers in the world figuring this, Fred."

Fred shook his head unhappily. "Sure. And they'd be right, if Wickman hadn't got the third tube blasting at the end. They're figuring this on the power of two motors only. That must have been all Poorhouse noticed before it cut below his horizon. They've extrapolated from early coördinates and what Poorhouse saw. Dr. Sessions, was that ship decelerating steadily?"

"No." Sessions considered it slowly, then spoke more firmly. "No, it wasn't. Its exhaust seemed to flicker and grow stronger, as you described it before."

"Exactly. Nobody would think Wickman would risk spinning the ship, but he did it—and he got his third tube working. That means he was falling a lot more slowly than they figured. They can't reach the right spot from those figures."

He tried to explain the change that would carry the ship farther across the surface before it landed, drawing a rough sketch on a piece of paper. It made enough sense to the others for them to realize he might be right, even though they couldn't follow the mathematics of a landing course easily. Just as their technical geological discussions gave him only the general idea behind the words, so the jargon of plotting was beyond their full understanding. They understood enough to become gravely worried.

Sessions studied the sketch and finally threw it back on the desk. "I'll back your judgment most of the way on this, Fred. Mona, can you get a signal through to the Station?"

"With this transmitter?" She snorted. "Unless they put a tight beam antenna on us, we'd be far down under solar noise. Even maser amplifiers can't pull intelligence out of such a mess. . . . Okay, I'll try. I hope Wonderboy knows what he's talking about."

Sessions' voice was flat. "I have reason to believe Mr. Halpern's ability saved the *Kepler* after your repairs on the computer failed, Dr. Williams. I suggest you try calling the Station."

She obviously didn't approve, but she went to work. Fred had no reason to complain about her efforts. After nearly an hour of steady signaling, there was still no response.

It wasn't surprising. Their transmitter had been designed for a limited range, unlike the sets in the ships, or the larger installation at Emmett Base. Gantry's rescue party would probably carry a ship transmitter and receiver to keep in touch with the Station, but the expedition hadn't felt it necessary.

Perhaps it didn't matter. Fred had never fully convinced anyone on the Station of his mental plotting ability, and they'd probably disregard his ideas. The only one who had ever completely accepted the idea had been a psychologist at the Academy, who claimed the talent was not unknown in other fields. Spacemen would hardly consult a psychologist about space orbits and plotting.

Sessions had been pondering silently during the fitful discussion going on while they tried to contact the Station. He signaled Mona to stop trying.

"We've got to do whatever we can," he told the group. "I'm afraid that isn't much. There's at least one chain of unknown mountains between us and the location Fred suggests for the crash. We don't even have photos of it to suggest a pass. It looks a lot worse than anything we've come through, and by the time we could get there, it might be dark. I won't risk the men and equipment here on anything less than certainty."

"I'm certain of where they are," Fred insisted.

"I'm sure you are—and you may be right. But if you're even twenty miles off, we'd miss them in the dark, and that's a lot smaller error than you claim the Station made. Be reasonable, Fred. I'm admitting you're good, but you plotted that exhaust against a horizon without knowing how much the horizon deviates from its theoretical height. There are dozens of factors that could lead to errors. Do you deny that?"

"No, sir." He'd thought of all those things himself, and he was still sure he knew where the ship had landed. He was also sure he couldn't convince the others; if he insisted too much, they'd be less likely to believe him than if he seemed reasonable.

"It's out of the question to attempt a rescue directly," Sessions went on.

"Maybe a single tractor . . ." Fred began.

The leader cut him off shortly. "No! A single tractor is taking too much risk if anything goes wrong. I'm not breaking up the group. We can travel light, and we'll travel together."

"Then you're going to try to make it?" Mike Boland asked.

The older man shook his head. "No, it's impossible. But we might be able to get back to the area where the Station plotted the crash. We know that trail thoroughly. We can get there as soon as Gantry can make it. We'll start broadcasting to his group, and let them put through a call to the Station with Fred's ideas."

Surprisingly it was Mona Williams who voiced the first approval. "All right, if we're going to gamble, that makes sense. We can even help investigate the area. If the Station plotting is wrong, we'll be able to prove it. Then they'll have to listen to Halpern's ideas."

Sessions nodded. It was obvious that the same idea had occurred to him.

It might make sense, but it wouldn't work, Fred felt. There would be a delay while the expedition was rounded up and made ready; beyond that, there would be wasted time while the tractors and trailers backtracked to the official disaster site, waited for confirmation from the Station, and finally headed toward the real location of the ship. It would probably take eight days or more. That was a long time to expect Wickman and Ramachundra to hold on—too long.

On the other hand, a single tractor might make off at top speed, taking more risks than a full expedition could afford. With luck, it should find the ship in three days, while there was daylight for scouting around, if necessary. That was still not good, but men could survive for that long under some pretty rough conditions.

"Dr. Sessions," he asked, "can I see you in the tractor?"

Sessions glanced at him in surprise, but nodded. The leader was giving orders for striking the camp and picking up the men who were out on projects as far as fifty miles away.

Ten minutes later, the scientist joined Fred in the tractor. "Well, Fred?"

It was now or never, Fred realized. If he had proposed his idea in front of the group, they might think he was trying to get credit and looking for glory, as he'd been accused of doing before. His only chance was to present his plan to Sessions alone.

It was hard to outline the logic of his idea, though he was sure the use of a single tractor was far better than the plan they had agreed on. He drew out the incomplete maps of the area where Wickman must be and began pointing out possible routes, indicating the time it would take.

Sessions shoved them aside wearily. He looked unhappy and tired, but his voice was firm.

"No, Fred, it's out of the question. I won't order a man to commit suicide; that wouldn't do Wickman any good. The odds against a single man are too heavy. What would you have done in the dust pit alone? Or Whitley on that ledge? The Moon isn't a one-man proposition."

"The first landing I made here was a one-boy operation," Fred told him hotly. He regretted the words as soon as they were out; it was too late to call them back.

Sessions grinned, seizing on them. "To be sure. So I've heard. And if I remember the story, you came down in the ship all right, then turned over. The ship landed on the air lock, and you couldn't get out. Three men might have dug out, but one couldn't. So you had to wait until a real group expedition arrived. Do you really want to use that as an example?"

Fred shook his head unhappily. Yet he couldn't give up. "Then send someone like Boland. He's level-headed. He'll make out if anyone can."

"No." Sessions stood up and began pacing about the tiny space not filled with supplies. "No, if I were sending anyone, I'd pick you. Surprise you? Well, it's true. You're just fool enough to make it where a sane man might not. No one is going alone. No one! Is that clear?"

"Yes, sir."

Sessions snorted. "Don't give me a 'yessir' in that tone of voice, Mr. Halpern. I'm still running this expedition. I think we had a little talk before you joined up. We discussed mutiny then, didn't we? You remember the penalty possible for disobeying my orders?"

At the moment, Fred didn't care to remember; it had been something about execution for mutiny. That didn't matter to him.

"Are you refusing me the right to go, sir?" he asked formally.

Sessions' lips tensed in a straight line. "Do I have to? Use your own judgment for a change," he suggested. "Now, will you get this tractor ready for the trip back?"

Fred nodded tensely and turned to the controls. The older man hesitated for a moment, then grabbed his shoulder and spun him around.

"Fred," Sessions said, "I know how important this is. I know how you feel about the colonists, your father, that ship out there. Give me a little credit, too. I feel it just as much as you do. So let's both stop bristling at each other, shall we? I thought we were friends. How about it?"

In spite of himself, Fred felt a smile spread over his face. He took the other's outstretched hand, and the smile deepened. "Sorry, Dr. Sessions. I guess I'm still reacting to the whole trouble. I'm not angry."

Sessions grinned back and clapped him fondly on the shoulder before heading for the air lock. The smile lingered on Fred's face as the older man passed back to the laboratory. Then the boy swung back to study the tractor.

He really wasn't angry, but he hadn't changed his mind. He had no doubts about what he must do. Maybe Wickman and Ramachundra were dead already. Maybe his father would be broken, whether or not the ship was found. Maybe the World Congress representative couldn't help the colony, even if he survived. None of those things mattered. The simple fact was that two men might be alive and badly injured; he knew where they were and had a chance to rescue them. He had to take the chance.

Anyone who wanted could call it mutiny and do whatever they chose to him afterward. That was the way it would have to be.

The tractor was stocked with as much material as it could carry. There was the maximum supply of fuel. The cabin held medical supplies, spare oxygen tanks, food, water, and even a single-man pressure tent of plastic. It was equipped to meet any emergency, and there was little else he could think to take.

He glanced at the mirror that showed him the rest of the camp. There was no one around the tractor; the two other tractors were not occupied at the moment. Sessions had climbed back into the laboratory. The simplest way to desert was simply to leave—there would never be a better opportunity than he had now.

He reached for the control levers and jammed full power into the motor. The tractor spun about sharply, turning to face north and east. Then the two treads began whipping around their tracks together, and the machine was driving away from the camp at its top speed.

There was a sputtering from the radio. Fred reached forward and snapped it off quickly. He had no desire to argue. He tried not to see the men spilling out of the laboratory, making frantic gestures toward him.

It came to him that he was leaving the only group

where he'd ever earned a real place for himself by his own merits. He'd spent his whole life looking for honest acceptance, it seemed, and now he was giving it up. That mattered to him, but it couldn't stop him.

CHAPTER 15 /

Crack-up

THE FIRST few minutes presented the only danger to Fred's chance to get away. A man could outrun the tractor, even at its top speed, for a mile or two in this light gravity. It would have been possible to stop him, but no one seemed to think of that. He drove on steadily at maximum speed until the little camp was out of sight behind him.

Things would be more difficult for them without this tractor, but the two remaining would still permit them to finish their work and return to Base. At least he wasn't endangering them by running off.

He slowed down a little after the first miles, trying to find the best speed possible without wasting fuel. The tractor would have to operate at a higher average speed than had been intended by its makers. He could only hope that the repairs would stand up under the steady racing.

The sun was in the west, a few days before setting, and the shadows were lengthening. The dust was charged with static, dancing off the surface and making it hard to see. He was taking risks with every mile he covered; that was another thing that couldn't be helped. If he slowed down to a sensible pace, it would be much too late by the time he located the ship.

There was no chance to spot the pits and irregularities in the surface while the dust was suspended by the static charge. A wide and deep fissure would show, but none of the expected irregularities. He drove on, taking his chances.

Several times he felt the tractor sinking. It would lose speed as the dust spun under the treads, but the silicone rubber never completely lost traction. All he could hope was that the pit he was entering did not have sharp sides and plow ahead as steadily as possible. In that, he seemed to be lucky. The tractor sank below the top of the roof in several of the pits, but eventually it emerged and went forward again. In one pit he found a rise on the other side that was too steep for the machine. He was able to turn and ascend it at an angle.

He locked the controls in place and hunted up water and food concentrates once, keeping his eye on the trail ahead as much as possible. Eventually he would have to take breaks to rest himself, but he wanted to avoid any stops while he was reasonably fresh.

He'd begun to realize that it might have been better to get another man to go with him. Boland would probably have been willing; one could have managed to sleep while the other drove. Then he rejected the idea. He had been right, after all. The tractor carried a certain amount of oxygen and other equipment, and one man would use less than two; this would leave more for the use of Wickman and Ramachundra if they needed it.

He felt the tractor jounce while he was eating. Its treads spun and then seemed to lock. The tractor tilted backward. Fred fed it the last bit of power. Slowly, the machine inched ahead, caught, and went lurching forward again.

He'd hit a faulty section of crust. It was another danger, since much of the Moon had hollows and pits on or just under the crust. There was no point in reducing speed, since he had a better chance of getting past while the tractor was moving fast enough to cover the break before it could fall in.

The strain and steady concentration began to tell on him sooner than he had expected. Driving looked easy enough, but it was one of the toughest jobs he had ever mastered. He had to fight against himself as well as the machine; there was a constant temptation to let his attention wander or to gaze blindly at the distance; such habits could be fatal.

He gave up and came to a stop, to eat another hasty meal of concentrates. There was no hope of avoiding sleep, he realized. He glanced at his watch and sat giving himself orders to wake up in four hours, trying to drive the message so deep that he'd remember, even in his sleep. Sometimes he had that trick of waking himself on schedule, but he didn't trust himself too far.

It seemed to work, however. He woke about fifteen minutes before he had ordered himself to, according to his watch; he was still too tired to feel he'd slept long enough. Probably the trick of timing worked better under pressure.

The shadows grew larger as the sun dropped further to the west. The terminator was steadily moving westward toward him, as he moved somewhat eastward to meet it. With any luck, he'd be at his destination sometime before darkness fell abruptly. To make up for the difficulty in seeing the terrain ahead against the harsh shadows, he began to steer toward ground above the level of the worst dust. The ground was rougher, and strewn with outcroppings of rock, yet less troublesome than the shadows made it seem.

He was making good time, he realized. Before he stopped for sleep again because of his inability to concentrate on driving, he was on the first rising slope that led to the mountains he had to cross. He stopped to eat and study them, comparing them with what little detail showed on the map. There were three places where they seemed to be broken, where there might be a pass. This was actually an extension of the range through which the expedition had first forced its way; it was a major chain of mountains that swept in a great curve, and going around it seemed impossible.

He put off his decision until after he had slept another four hours and could study the problem with a clearer mind. Then he decided that there was no obvious choice. He headed toward the nearest crack in the great, rugged peaks. Some of the mountains made any on Earth seem like pigmy models, but there were places where ancient breaks seemed to separate the towering peaks. The one he was approaching looked good from the little that showed on the map.

Traveling was easy at first. He pushed on for several miles at a fair speed. The sunlight faded quickly as the peaks threw their shadows over the gorges and breaks; even by headlight the going was not too bad. Then there was a section where he had to hunt his way slowly. He was beginning to congratulate himself on his choice when the trail came to a sudden end against a hopelessly unscalable rock wall.

There was only one thing to do. He backed to a place where there was a chance to climb up for a survey, took the powerful portable searchlight, and went out in his suit. He was again aware of the need of another man. One slip could mean the end of his rescue attempt—and of himself. He climbed carefully, searching for each step and testing each foothold. Halfway up the sloping wall of rock, he gave up. Even from that height, he could see by the beam of his light that this was a dead end, with no possible path ahead.

Back in the tractor, he managed to turn and begin the return trip. He studied every inch, swinging the headlight about, but there seemed to be no alternative. Finally he came through the cleft and was on the outer slope again.

The next possibility lay fifteen miles away; he had wasted almost four hours on the first attempt. There was no use worrying about that. All he could do was try again—keep trying until he found some way through the mountains. He was forced to realize that there might be no passage—these were not Earth mountains, where rivers and millions of years of weathering had worn regular passes; on the Moon, any pass must be considered a lucky accident, until men could come here in sufficient numbers to blast trails from solid rock.

The next entrance to the forbidding barrier was disappointing at first. He hesitated, wondering whether it might not be better to go on to the third possibility. Then he shrugged, and pointed the machine forward. There was a hint of lighter shadow far ahead that might prove to be a cleft through which he could make his way.

The first mile was almost impossible. The tractor labored up and down, twisting its way along small ledges and through narrow gaps. Once he had to get out and climb over the tractor to get to a boulder blocking his passage. He struggled and fought against it with a heavy bar of metal, barely able to budge it. There was blasting powder in the tractor, but he dared not use it for fear of starting a rock slide. When the stone finally rolled aside, he was shaking with exhaustion.

Then the gap he was following opened a little, where he had seen the faint reflection of light from the upper peaks. It continued to grow wider for some time, and he breathed more easily. The widening indicated that it might be the end of some great cleavage which pierced through the mountains. Boulders and broken rock had fallen from above, cracked away by the heating and cooling of day and night; the rock had partly filled the great chasm, making a passable floor on which the tractor slowly crawled and wriggled its way.

It was treacherous, though. He could never be sure that some great slab of stone was not so precariously balanced that his passage would send it hurtling away under him. He had to hold down his speed, even when the way seemed clear. More time was spent testing his way than traveling. The places where he had to use maximum power to climb some obstacle were too frequent. It meant using more peroxide fuel than he liked, but there was no help for it.

At the top of one long rise, he saw a tiny slit beyond which there seemed to be open ground. He couldn't be sure, but it gave a lift to his sagging spirits. He'd been going on nerve for the last few hours. If he could see the plains beyond, it meant the mountains were narrower here than the map indicated.

A half hour later, he was sure of it. He had reached the top of the climb through the gorge, and was moving down a fairly straight break in the great walls. Ahead definitely lay the lighted horizon of the plains. The going was easier, too. He relaxed for a few minutes.

He should have known better than to believe it was all over. As he came around a slight curve onto another stretch of descending trail, his headlights spotted a break in the path running from wall to wall of the gorge. It was a small fissure, as such things went, but wider than the length of the tractor, and impossible to maneuver, as far as he could see.

He got out wearily, picking his way cautiously across the rock and broken slabs under him, and drew near the edge. He tested it with his bar, trying to find whether the edge was sound, before going closer.

The sides of the break seemed solid and strong; he gained confidence as he stared down. It looked as if a quake had dropped one edge of the trail a couple of feet below the other, leaving him on the higher edge. He might even be able to reach the bottom. For that matter, he could leap across easily enough with the lunar gravity, although it would do no good to try going on without the tractor. He couldn't backtrack and try another pass. His fuel was holding up fairly well, but it would never last for the return through the mountains and still another attempt.

The lower section of the trail across the split was

smooth enough, he saw. Once the tractor was across, there would be no further trouble from that.

The only solution was to jump the tractor across it.

He estimated it. At maximum speed, the machine would be traveling forward fifteen feet every second. It would fall less than three feet the first second, and drop steadily faster after that. The downward slope of the trail would cancel out some of the difference in height between the two edges. He lacked enough speed to make it.

He considered the jump again; it was so close that, the idea kept coming back, while his mind insisted there was no other way. The tractor might not stand the landing, yet he was fairly sure the shock would not be too great; the treads would soak up most of it. All he needed was a slightly upward lift before leaving the higher edge.

Then he nodded to himself. There were enough rocks and fragments he could move. The only hope was to build a mound of them, like the upsweep at the edge of a ski jump, and hope they would stand the momentary impact of the tractor.

He fell to, dragging rocks into place and trying to wedge them firmly with smaller pieces. The largest had to go at the edge—these required the firmest bracing. There was a long, carefully graded slope of smaller rubble to be built behind it. He was sweating and panting in his suit, and his oxygen was running low before he finished. He put the last touches on it and climbed back into the tractor. He was hungry and thirsty. He couldn't stop to eat; if he stopped now, he might lose his nerve.

Slowly he backed the machine up the slope as far as he thought necessary. He gunned the motor, letting the clutches slip. There was no chance to stop and try this again. He had to hit the edge at full speed and keep going.

Abruptly he let the clutches engage fully. The tractor bucked and lurched forward, picking up speed, while he fought to hold it in a straight path over the rubble. It seemed to thunder down the last few feet and out onto the ramp he had built. Stones ground and pitched under the treads. He had no time for worry about that.

The front of the treads touched the edge. The tractor seemed to settle, but the lift at the end of the ramp held. There was a final lurch, then a feeling of total ease as the machine left the path completely and was over the open chasm, while the treads spun without resistance.

The shock of landing made his ankles ache, and the tractor groaned. The motor bucked, and the treads jerked to a stop that must have ripped half the clutch lining away. The rear of the machine sagged, still over the edge of the split.

Then momentum and the savage biting of the treads carried the machine forward. He'd made it.

He let the motor die and sagged over the controls, breathing heavily until he got enough control of himself to grope for food and water. He wasn't hungry now, but he forced himself to eat and relax before picking up the trail downward and out of the mountains.

The rest of the way was easy. Before he realized it, he was on the flatter plains, still in the shadow of the mountains. The hungry, gigantic teeth of the mountains yawned emptily behind him.

He forced himself to sleep here, briefly and for the final time. By the time he would need sleep again, he would either have found the ship or have failed. In spite of all the setbacks, he was making as good time as he'd hoped. He'd reach the ship—if it was there—on the thirty-sixth day "after Base," just three days from the time he'd left the expedition camp.

It was harder to wake this time; he'd been getting too little sleep, and the fatigue was mounting. Still, the prospect of reaching his goal helped to lift the fog from his mind.

He crossed the plains, back into the area of full light. The sun was two days from setting. It was off to his side and slightly behind him, and mercifully offered no glare. He came to a small crater, driving the tractor up the crater wall, down into the depression, and across it to the far wall. It was a normal crater, probably produced by a meteorite of only a few thousand tons, without even a single smaller crater inside the main, ancient one. Earth had once had such craters; time and weather had filled in most of them.

Abruptly he stopped the tractor, but it was too late. He climbed out, examining the ground under the front treads. He had glimpsed what looked like another cluster of tiny plants, but the treads had demolished all life, if there had been any. He could see one tiny fragment; it shattered and became dust as he watched.

He couldn't have collected specimens. He had no idea of how to save them; certainly the air inside the tractor would ruin them. There was no time to stop and search for more.

He kept his eyes carefully directed to the ground after that, but there were no more signs of life.

Hours later, he came to the area he had selected on the map as the site of the crash. It was a bowl-like crater, with one wall on the far side blending into a rocky escarpment. He gunned the motor, climbing the slope up to the crater, his eyes aching to look for signs of the ship.

It was there, he saw as he reached the top. Or the wreck of it was there, out toward the center of the small crater. Long before he reached it, he could see that the landing had been a brutal one. The whole tail section was crumpled into accordion folds where it had sagged in on itself. It had tilted, too, and lay on its side.

As he drew up to it, he could see that the front of the control cabin had been ripped out by the force of the crack-up. The entire ship must be open to the vacuum of the Moon.

CHAPTER 16 /

False Hopes

AT FIRST GLANCE, the ship looked as if no human body could have stood the shock of the landing. As Fred circled it slowly, he could see that the shock seats were empty—that meant someone had to have been alive to release the straps. He cut around the nose of the ship into the area of dark shadow behind it. Just as he flicked on his headlight, a figure sprang up before him.

Fred jerked the tractor to a halt and went out through the lock as quickly as possible. In the light, he could see Dr. Ramachundra, clad in a spacesuit three sizes too large. The flopping figure looked ludicrous, but the voice over the radio was as gay as Fred remembered.

"Ah, yes. Mr. Halpern, how nice of you to come. I was telling poor Major Wickman only a little while ago . . ."

"Where is he? How is he?" Fred cried.

Then the answer came with a chuckle that sounded weak but was all too familiar. "Well, well, the Moonboy. Our hero rides again. Did you bring the reporters with you?"

Fred saw the pilot. He lay in a depression partly filled with dust so that it almost covered his suit. With the sun shining into the unprotected cabin, the ship must have become too hot, driving them out in the open and into the shadow. Out of the sun, the ground cooled far too quickly. The little dust pit was the logical solution, since the dust made an excellent insulator.

Ramachundra was fussing around excitedly, seemingly not bothered by the clumsy suit. "Major Wickman would not relax. Oh, no. Not as I showed him. He does not trust yoga. Now, behold. Four broken ribs and a broken arm, I believe. The medical kit was lost in the wreck, so I have been hopeless to help. It is good you are here. Indeed, it is."

Fred bent over, but Wickman motioned him away. "I can carry myself. We're all heroes here, you know."

He managed to shake himself out of the dust and get to his feet. Fred shrugged and let the man stalk stubbornly through the air lock. When they were all inside the tractor, he dragged out the medical kit while Ramachundra helped the pilot out of his suit. Fortunately, the first aid course at the Academy was a stiff one. Fred found a box of pain remedy and gave three pills to Wickman, along with a standard precautionary injection of antibiotics. Then he began stalling for time until the pills could take effect.

"How'd you manage the landing, anyhow? I saw the ship start spinning, then I lost it."

"Time for bedtime stories while the hero plays doctor, eh?" Wickman asked. "All right. I can take it—anything you say."

His account was similar to what Fred had guessed at the beginning. They'd been forced to rush against time before the ship could be ordered back to Earth, so the big rocket tube liners had been given only a hasty inspection. The rockets had worked at the start, but when landing operations began, one tube had blown. The only hope of making a landing was by spinning the ship. During the final moments, Wickman had tried blinking his eyes, opening them briefly during each spin of the ship, in order to cut through the blur of motion and get a fixed view of the ground. The trick must have worked; he'd landed at much too high a speed, but otherwise perfectly. Then a second tube had blown, throwing the ship on its side.

Fred whistled when the pilot finished the account. "Nobody else could have handled such a job. It was magnificent piloting," he said honestly.

Wickman stared at him in surprise, then shrugged. "Thanks. Now, how come you're the one man on this whole world to reach us?"

This time, when Fred finished his report, it was Wickman's turn to whistle softly. "So your mental computer really works. I guess I don't have to say I'm glad it does. We were down to six hours of oxygen apiece when you turned up." He grinned suddenly. "Pretty hot course plotting, Mr. Halpern. Now you'd better get on with me. I'll be able to take it."

He took it, though his face turned gray when the tape was wrapped around the injured chest and sweat popped out on his forehead while his arm was being set. Somehow, he kept the silent grin on his lips. That smile had probably been frozen there as he watched the last six hours of oxygen begin to trickle away without knowing whether anyone could reach them in time. While he was waiting for the plastic cast to set, he picked up the questioning again.

"So, when do we set out to meet the main rescue party?"

Fred considered. The trip would be a little rough on the pilot, but not too bad. At least there were no mountains to cross before the rendezvous with Dr. Sessions and Gantry in the officially chosen area. There was no point in delaying.

"We'd better start as soon as I can refuel. I'll need time to draw peroxide from your motor pump tanks. I'm down to a few gallons of peroxide in the tractor. That shouldn't take too long." He stopped as he saw their faces. "What's the matter?"

Dr. Ramachundra pointed outside. Fred swung the headlight to follow the motion. Then he grunted with disgust. The ship had taken the greatest strain where the peroxide tank had been located. The area was now mashed almost as flat as if there had never been a tank there. Obviously there was not a drop of peroxide left. While Fred had a little fuel, it was not half enough to reach the rendezvous with the other rescuers.

They'd have to stay here until they could be rescued by Gantry. At least the effort Fred had made wasn't all wasted; without his arrival, he reminded himself, the two men couldn't have survived.

Now, though, there was going to be the problem of shelter. The one-man pressure tent was too small for all of them. The tractor cab was big enough, but it presented other troubles. When the motor was running it gave off enough heat to maintain warmth inside the tractor. When the motor was off, heat was provided by a trickle of fuel that warmed tubing under the floor. They couldn't afford that waste now. Unless the tractor could be insulated somehow, it offered no protection against the coming night and subfreezing temperatures.

"I'd better look for salvage in the ship," he decided.

Wickman had been through too much already, and seemed glad to be left alone, but Ramachundra bobbed along beside Fred. The ship was an incredible shambles; nearly everything in the cabin was ruined. There was one large tank of oxygen, unsuitable for coupling to the suits. He sent the little man back to the tractor with that. He found one corner of the freight hold open enough for him to reach in. There was a box of the incredibly strong glue used by the colonists to cement and repair the plastic for their hothouse. It might serve to cement insulation to the tractor cab's walls, since it could weld things together with the strength of steel. He dragged it out and went to inspect the insulation in the ship hull, where rips exposed it. The stuff was so thoroughly cemented that removing it was impossible. He turned to the radio, to see that a framing girder had collapsed across it, rendering it useless.

Ramachundra had returned and stood beaming at the edge of the crater and the cliffs through an opening in the hull. "A strange and fascinating world, Mr. Halpern. Yes. I went exploring, even to the little cliffs. One learns to walk here, even in such a suit as this. Fascinating. Indeed, yes. There are caves there—like bubbles. Strange to find caves on the Moon where no men could use them, is it not?"

"Yeah," Fred admitted absently. He'd puzzled over the mystery of the bubble caves; no one knew exactly what caused them. Then he jerked to attention at the idea that hit him. He grabbed up the box of cement and motioned the little man after him, hurrying toward the tractor.

As they drew up beside one cave Fred had spotted from a distance, he realized they were in luck, for a change. The cavern was a little ten-foot bubble with a small section in front broken open to form an entrance. The floor curved, not too badly, and there seemed to be no breaks in the hard, smooth walls. Except for the entrance, it was probably airtight. The entrance hole, with a little enlarging, would just hold the little air lock section of the pressure tent. If that could be fastened in place with the cement, they'd have shelter far better than a tent, since the rock would serve as adequate insulation, holding an average temperature somewhere between the burning day and the freezing night.

The air lock was an ingeniously simple device, consisting of a man-sized pocket of two sections of clear plastic. When one side was unzipped, a man could step in. It had to be zipped up again before the next section could be opened. The plastic clung to the suits so tightly that almost no oxygen would be lost in going in and out. Fred cut the tent, leaving plenty of overlap for the cement to hold it to the rock surface inside the bubble, and began fastening it in place while Dr. Ramachundra transferred the supplies from the tractor to the inner cave.

It took about half an hour for the plastic cement to harden, before they could turn on oxygen and fill the little cave. There was no sign of air loss.

Wickman had been using his good arm to cut up the rest of the tent, shaping the foam insulation into pads to serve as beds. He had also rigged up a light, powered by a battery, and was working on the chemical pans that would soak up carbon-dioxide. Fred dropped onto one of the pads to rest for a moment before helping finish the job. His eyes were burning, and his head felt light and hot. He put it down on his arms to rest for a second. . . .

It was still light outside when he woke, but he could tell that he'd been asleep for quite a while. The strain and lost sleep had finally caught up with him. There was no sense regretting it; he'd needed the rest. He saw that Wickman was also asleep, groaning faintly from the pain of his ribs. Dr. Ramachundra was sitting at the plastic section, staring out, with a tray of food beside him.

"Another world," the little man said, and his face was curiously lighted from within. "Ah, Fred—if I may call you that? Yes. Ah, Fred, when I was your age, this was not even a dream to me. But inside was a longing. And now, I have crossed space and am here. It is indeed worth living for this."

"Worth nearly dying for?" Fred asked.

"Worth fully dying for. Oh, worth more than that."

"I'm sure the colonists and Governor Gantry will be glad to hear that. They were afraid you might be opposed to colonizing here."

Ramachundra sighed. "Yes. Without me, the World Congress would already have helped the colony. I have been the opponent to the plan, the one who kept it from being voted for favorably among the independent nations. That is why they sent me, hoping to convince me."

He launched into a tale of a struggle that had gone on

for years. The independent nations had watched the United States quietly take over the Moon, though without official claims. They had dreaded the idea of space being settled by any one nation or group of nations. It should be fully international. When they saw interest fail on Earth, they detected a chance to step in, by recognizing the Moon as an independent nation. There were huge funds, available for aid to new nations. That was why they had also ordered three of the new-type ships to be built for them. But Ramachundra had always managed to get enough votes to prevent any resolution being adopted.

"Why?" Fred asked. The man was obviously in love with space. His actions made no sense.

"Violence!" The little man spat the word out. "I dreamed of new worlds where men could be free of animal violence. Then I saw men go out into space, and not only did violence go with them, but it increased. Yes, it grew worse. Space makes men more violent. You were violent in rushing here once, and the men who followed were violent in their haste. Those colonists—they attack the Moon to beat it into their mold, like savage men taming a savage beast. This rescue—a violent revolt against your leader, was it not? Even when you meet Major Wickman, violence flows between you at once. Fred, I *hate* violence. Yes, hate. I resent the violence that makes me feel so violent against it. No, I cannot help in such a conquest of space."

Fred grimaced bitterly to himself. A lot of good he'd done the colony by helping to save the one man who could defeat them. Yet he couldn't bother thinking of that. He had a lot of violent work ahead of him, he realized.

The sun was almost over the horizon as he trudged toward the ship rather than use the tractor and its precious bit of fuel. He carried a metal bar, striking the ground with it at each step. Why had his father bothered to send Ramachundra? Had he thought the sight of the colony would change the man's prejudices? It didn't seem probable. The colony *was* violent—it had to have a sort of violent fanaticism to survive at all. Worlds could never be won without violence.

He went through as much of the ship as he could, prying out sections with the bar, looking for radio repair parts. He found them, half ruined by the buckling of the walls. He could only hope they would do. Then he pried out the radio and a set of batteries. Getting the antenna loose from outside the hull was harder. Eventually, he had everything, and headed back to the shelter of the cave, after leaving a marker near the ship pointing the way.

Wickman was awake, quiet and obviously in some pain. He realized the importance of signaling the Station as much as Fred, and joined in going over the set. The radios in the suits and in the tractor were useless; they had a range of only a few miles and could not tune to the Station frequencies. Communication depended on getting this set fixed.

The receiver was only in fair shape. The transistors and integrated circuits were all right, but the printed circuit board had been broken, ruining the connections and some parts. Wickman worked on that while Fred dug into the mess that had been the transmitter.

"I can jury-rig this," Wickman said finally. "No knowing how long it will last, but some of these parts will hold up under overload for a while. Need them?"

Fred shook his head. The voltages in the transmitter were higher, and the components Wickman had picked were useless for his needs. He saw the pilot finish the repairs and connect the receiver to the antenna that had been mounted on the rocks above and coupled by a lead-in that ran through a sleeve in the tent plastic. There was a hiss of static, but no signals. It was impossible to tell whether it was really working, since the Station would hardly be broadcasting all the time.

They turned it on from time to time, while Fred

fought with the complexities of the transmitter. He knew basic radio theory, of course, but this was highly advanced circuitry, and he had no real test instruments.

He stopped to sleep when his hands began trembling with fatigue. When he awoke, the lunar night had dropped over the crater. Ramachundra was out somewhere, apparently watching the stars from the surface of the Moon. Wickman shook his head at the transmitter; he'd obviously tried to help but been unable to. "No messages," he said.

It was hours later when Fred gave up. There were ruined parts in the transmitter for which he could work out no substitutes. Their only hope was that Dr. Sessions would convince the Station to order Gantry north to find them. For a brief moment, Fred wondered whether Sessions would have made the trip, once Fred took off; he knew it was just pessimism getting out of hand. The scientist would do everything he could, just as Fred had tried what he felt best.

Abruptly, Wickman grunted. Something was coming over the receiver. It wasn't behaving as well as it should have done, and there was a great deal of noise in the background. But words were coming out, carrying a message beamed to the Moon from the Station. It seemed to be an argument with the rescue parties over the news Dr. Sessions had given. The receiver could not pick up the signal from the rescuers, and the one-sided conversation gave little information. There was a long period of silence.

"Calling Governor Gantry," the radio finally said. "If cross-checking original site shows no evidence of ship *Cosmic Egg,* a new search will be authorized on the basis of added information. We'll put it through the computers, allowing for added power and spin. Put young Halpern on."

There must have been quite a discussion of that, from what Fred could hear. Well, his father had to know sooner or later that he'd mutinied. It might as well be now.

It was over two hours later when the Station acknowledged the failure of the preliminary search and began sending down new lunar coördinates. Fred listened casually at first, then banged his fists brutally against his head, as if to change the words pouring out of the speaker.

The new destination was more than forty miles southeast of where they were—too far to reach by the tractor with its tiny supply of fuel.

Dr. Sessions had been unable to understand his mathematics well enough to convince the Station, and they'd figured their own orbit on the basis of false coördinates from the ship transmitter and a lower spin and release of power from the rocket tubes than Wickman had used.

From the final sign-off, Fred realized the rescue teams were accepting the Station plotting instead of believing what he said. Eventually, when they failed to find the ship, they might turn back to this crater where Fred had marked the crash on the laboratory maps. By then, it would be too late.

There wasn't enough oxygen to supply the little cave shelter until such a delayed rescue could reach them.

CHAPTER 17/

Life or Death

FRED SAT staring through the plastic entrance at the darkness outside for a few minutes. He had no right to blame anyone, he realized. If Wickman had told him a landing could be made here under the existing conditions and that men could walk away from it, he'd have refused to believe him. No man could have such faultless coördination of nerves and muscles. Yet the pilot had known he did have them and relied on them without hesitation. Fred had no right to ask others to believe in a strange gift of his own, any more than he could have been asked to trust Wickman.

He got up to study the oxygen left. Counting the supplies from the tractor and the big tank from the ship, they might stretch it a little more than two more days, but not much more.

He got up and snapped on his spacesuit, heading for the lock. There was a physical need for exercise, to damp out some of the dark thoughts in his mind. He headed out aimlessly, keeping sight of the cave's lighted section to guide him back. It was a strange world here, he thought for the hundredth time. Something deep inside him liked it and the challenge it presented. Someday, somehow, men would take it over. He might have missed his chance, but there must be opportunity for others.

He had walked in a great arc when he headed back;

he could see the little cliffs on his left. The cave mouth was hidden now, but he could follow the rocks back. He moved along, flashing his light against the rocks.

The sight of the plants hit him without warning. He had come around an outcropping and flashed his light into a little ravine without thinking. Then he was staring at them—not one plant, or even a dozen; there must have been more than a hundred, spreading out, their odd little branches stretched to where the last sunlight had vanished.

There could be no doubt that they were plants. At the top of each was a little budding growth like a partly opened tulip, bearing no relation to anything crystalline. It could only be a spore sac, ready to dump the seeds of more life onto the surface of the Moon for another lunar day.

He stared at the growths, fascinated. There were no insects here to spread pollen, nor any winds to carry the seeds. The plants had found an answer of their own. The main stalk was bent like a bow, tensed to snap upright, tossing the spores outward. Like a bowstring, another filament of plant stretched down, holding the spore branch bent. It would hold until the cold of the night weakened it. Then, when the "string" snapped, the main branch would let go with enough force to throw the spores great distances.

He let out a yell in his helmet and went dashing toward the tractor. In there, he rummaged through the material that had not been needed in the cave until he found an empty plastic bottle and cap used for dust samples. It would serve equally well to keep the spores in a vacuum until they could be studied.

As he turned back, Ramachundra came out of the cave. Fred had no desire to talk. He headed back to the plants, pointing them out to the other.

Ramachundra dropped down as Fred settled before one of the plants with the opened bottle. "Ah, the mystery of life," the little man said. "Yes, the great mystery."

"Mystery and beauty," Fred said slowly. They were oddly beautiful in their adaptation to life here, he realized. Once he'd gotten used to their strangeness, their delicacy represented a queer beauty like none men had seen before.

Ramachundra looked up in mild surprise. "You see it, too? I am so glad, Fred. Yes, very glad. But why are you waiting?"

It was a good question. There was no need to wait, since a single flick of his finger could have snapped the string to release the spores into the bottle. It might be some time before the cold accomplished the same thing. But he shook his head stubbornly.

"These things have a hard enough time managing to live at all here. Let them alone until they're ready. They've earned every minute they can get."

Ramachundra chuckled softly, and said nothing more. Suddenly the little filament broke, the spore pod snapped forward and open, spraying an incredibly fine dark dust into the bottle. Others were popping as Fred sealed his collection, driving the spores even more forcefully than he had expected. Let them go. He had enough—probably millions—of the spores for all the testing and experimenting biologists could dream of, if anyone ever found the bottle.

He sealed it carefully and placed it in a hamper outside the tractor, where it would remain at the lunar surface temperature, scribbling a quick note in case it was found when he could no longer explain.

It could mean a lot to the Moon. It might mean filling the hopes of colonization and countless expeditions. That would have to remain a project for the future. He had other problems now.

Inside the cave, he reported his find to Wickman tersely. The pilot nodded; he had his own worries, too. He pointed to the receiver.

"Dead. It burned out a few minutes ago. We're out of touch permanently now, unless we can send up smoke signals."

Fred started to shrug, before the words hit him. Then he frowned. It might not work, but . . .

Wickman looked up, realizing the suggestion in his own words. "It might work," he said slowly. "It just might. Help me get my suit on."

"You're staying here. You're in no condition to do anything. Besides, this is a one-man job, and I thought of it first," Fred told him.

Wickman chuckled, and the grin came back to his lips. "Mr. Halpern, it's one-man suicide, if you're thinking what I'm thinking. I'm not in the best shape, but I'm not sure I can't give you the beating you've been asking for since I first knew you. Do I get help with this suit, or do I have to prove to you that I'm not a hopeless cripple?"

Ramachundra ran up to them, making unhappy clucking noises. Then, at the sight of their faces, he hesitated. A puzzled look came into his eyes and he stepped back, spreading his hands helplessly.

Getting the suit back on Wickman was a slow and painful business. Yet the pilot was right; it was a two-man job, if it were to be done properly. With Ramachundra hampered by a suit that made even seeing difficult, he was hardly the proper second man and would have to stay in the cave.

The two went out to the tractor together. Inside, Fred bent forward suddenly to help unfasten Wickman's helmet. Using one of the oxygen tanks here was wasteful, but they'd need a chance to confer properly. "I guess you're better at washing me out than I am at eliminating you," Fred said. "But you were always more clever about things than I was."

Wickman shook his head. "I wasn't being clever. I gave you every chance."

"That was the clever part," Fred admitted, putting

the tractor into motion and heading toward the ship. "You were too honest for words in front of Commandant Olson. You had him wrapped around your finger with all that honesty. But you didn't report all the needling you did."

"You're wrong. I reported that in detail, Mr. Halpern. I couldn't help reacting to you. You were the most arrogant and offensive student I ever had, with your pose of being a real spaceman among us earthlubbers. I could and did give him the whole background. Unfortunately, I thought you were also a liar and that you'd made that impossibly quick course alteration by wild luck. Otherwise, I'd have reported your insubordination and recommended that you be graduated in spite of it."

It was a small revelation to Fred that he'd probably been just as offensive as Wickman believed. He *had* considered himself a spaceman and the others as mere students, including Wickman. He'd seen only insult and cleverness in words which could just as easily have been taken as punctilious honesty. Well, now that he'd learned a little honesty himself, it was too late. He was the man supposed to be sent back to Earth, while Wickman was an accomplished spaceman.

Abruptly Wickman made a gesture of pushing something aside, and there was a touch of shyness to his grin. "My name is Sid," he said quietly. "Maybe we're both a little older, Fred."

"Maybe we are, Moon-boy," Fred acknowledged. Wickman looked startled, then laughed as he looked out at the Moonscape around them.

At the ship, Fred studied his plans again, comparing them with any ideas Wickman might have. They both decided on about the same course, except for one thing.

"Why worry about the ship?" Wickman asked.

"Salvage for the colony, maybe," Fred explained. "If the tractor will tow it, they can use it. Maybe they can patch it up to work and make fuel for it. If not, there's still a lot of material there."

Wickman accepted the idea without comment, and they went about their business.

Some of the monopropellant had dribbled out onto the surface from one of the tubes. It was a minor miracle that the landing shock hadn't broken the tanks while the rockets were still firing. It was safe enough now. Nothing but the heat of its own combustion or the blackened copper mesh used as a catalyst could set it off.

The main tank seemed not to have been ruined. Probably the liquid had acted as a shock absorber and served to protect it. Since the ship had carried fuel enough for a return as well as the trip here, there was a large amount of the material—probably more than they would need.

Fred attacked the side of the ship with the crowbar, battering and tugging at it until he could reach the motorized valves controlling the flow. They were not designed for manual operation; he had to enlarge the hole enough to get half inside the tank compartment and connect a battery directly to the motors. Then, protesting and stiff from being badly bent, the valve began to turn. It wouldn't open fully, but the fuel was moving out.

It ran slowly from one of the tubes, forming a thick river as it found a slight downward slope to the ground. Dark and oily in appearance, it spread under the headlights and began collecting in a pool where the ground dipped. Fred had no idea of how much would be needed. Better too much than too little, he decided.

Wickman drew back, holding the copper catalyst plate he had removed from the tube while Fred worked on the motor. There were probably fumes of the fuel around, since the vacuum caused any liquid to evaporate far more rapidly here than on Earth. He put the catalyst inside the tractor, where it couldn't possibly ignite the fuel and came out to watch as the little river gradually began to run dry while the pool filled.

Finding a way to hitch the tractor to the ship was another problem. Wickman solved it by suggesting they couple onto the twisted rocket tubes. The ship would be harder to drag tail first, but this was the only solution. There was enough cable in the tractor hampers.

The tractor was going to be almost useless, Fred realized, once this was over. The fuel supply was growing dangerously low. Well, it was really useless anyhow, and there was no point in trying to save peroxide now.

The motor growled unhappily as he eased in the clutches, and the treads protested as they tried to take up the load. Here on the Moon, the ship weighed one-sixth of what it would on Earth, but it had just as much inertia as anywhere else. This resistance to change of motion was the chief trouble. He began trying to twist it around, to overcome friction more easily. It seemed to make little difference.

Slowly, however, the great ship began to move behind them. They were probably damaging it a little more, but that couldn't be helped. It picked up speed, until the tractor was moving at almost three miles an hour, under the maximum force of the motor. Fred had wanted to drag it several miles away, but he abandoned the idea now. It should be reasonably safe at a mile from the pool of monopropellant.

He stopped and crawled out to unhitch the ship. The ride back was quicker, but it gave him time enough to go over his plans again, and he needed that.

Smoke signals. Well, they couldn't use smoke. Fire was another matter; the fuel produced one of the brightest, hottest flames possible from chemical reaction. All of it going off at once should be bright enough to light this whole section of the Moon. They were near the rim of the darkness of lunar night, but such a flare should be visible in the telescopes of the Station. It should last long enough for the astronomers to locate the source of the explosion accurately. There was no other way to communicate with the Station. Once the flame was observed, the Station could direct the rescue teams toward the right place. They might think men and ship had blown up together, but they'd come anyhow.

The problem was to time things so that the flare went off when the Station telescopes would probably be pointing at the Moon. With the expedition and Gantry looking for the ship, more than normal attention should be focused here, but the chances of the telescopes being on permanent lookout were not too good, with all the other important work to be done.

He wiped his forehead, trying to think. Days of strain and fatigue were beginning to cloud his judgment. Wickman didn't know enough of the Station schedule to help. All Fred could do was pick a time when the Station would be nearest the Moon in its orbit and hope.

Wickman was waiting beside the huge pool of fuel. His voice came over the radio. "Better put the copper screen in something before you hand it out, Fred. I'd hate to set this off until we get back a way."

"You're coming in to do the driving," Fred told him. "I'm the outside man."

"Nonsense. You're the tractor expert here."

"And I'm the man with an unbroken rib cage, Sid," Fred answered. "Figure it out. I can toss that catalyst twice as far as you can."

Wickman hesitated for a second; the logic of the argument could not be denied. He moved toward the air lock, walking slowly to favor his injured side. Fred helped him through the lock and began going over what little there was to learn about the controls for this operation. He let Wickman guide the tractor back clumsily until they were as far from the fuel as possible for their purpose.

It wasn't far enough, he knew. At the limit of his ability to throw the copper plate accurately, they were not fully outside the blast area. There was no air to carry the shock wave here. However, the exploding fuel would release its own tremendous outpouring of combustion gases, which would strike out savagely before they could be dissipated into the vacuum around them.

It was too late to worry now. He stopped to collect himself, then went out through the lock, to face the little lake of fuel.

He figured the trajectory of the plate more carefully than he'd figured any flight path before. His muscles seemed uncertain as he drew the plate back, but determination took over, sending a sudden spurt of confidence through him.

The plate sailed out of his hand and hurtled through the air, curving and falling slowly. He watched it for a fraction of a second, judging that the throw had been good. Then he darted for the air lock. The outer section came open . . .

A blaze of fire lighted the crater from edge to edge and rose up into the sky. The ground shook under a monstrous thunder of sound that leaped up through the air in his suit. Something like a heavy fist on his back drove Fred forward against the inner wall of the air lock. The tractor lurched under him as the pressure released.

He was half unconscious, dimly aware of a hand grasping and pulling at him. He felt himself being dragged, then dropped. There was a lucid moment when he was surprised that the tractor was moving, apparently undamaged. Then he was unconscious until Wickman's voice penetrated his ears.

"I'm all right," he managed to say. He tasted blood, and realized that his lip must have been bitten in the shock of the blast. His fingers came up to find another wound on his scalp.

He sat up abruptly finding himself in the cave, out of his suit, with Wickman busy attending to his cuts. Across the little room, Ramachundra sat watching, studying this further example of the violence of life here. The two must have dragged him in while he was unconscious.

"I'm all right," he repeated.

Wickman nodded. "Sure. No sign of concussion. You got a nasty blow, all the same, and you're going to rest before you talk any more. You've been dead on your feet for days, man."

Fred made no protest. There was nothing more they could do now, except wait while the oxygen disappeared slowly, and wonder whether their distress signal had been seen.

CHAPTER 18 /

Judgment

FRED AWOKE slowly. His head was thick at first, and the air seemed thin, hard to breathe. He groped his way up through a fog until bits of his memory came back.

The little cave was unchanged. Wickman was asleep on one of the beds, and Ramachundra sat cross-legged, writing on a pad that lay on his lap. There was no sign of a rescue party.

"How much longer?" he asked softly.

Ramachundra looked up, smiling faintly. There was no look of worry on the little man's face; instead, he seemed to be at perfect peace with himself. "About three more hours of oxygen, I believe. Our friend is sleeping to use less. And I have been using weak breathing while I wrote. It is a part of an ancient knowledge that needs no sleep. Indeed, yes."

He rose, putting the pad aside, and brought over a plastic plate of food and a cup of bouillon, barely warmed on the electric plate. Fred found that he was ravenously hungry. He felt almost himself again.

Three hours. It was strange and somehow unreal to know that there was so little time left to hope for rescue. The search party should have arrived long before this if his signal had been spotted. Either something had delayed them or the explosion had gone unnoticed. Well, the three in the cave couldn't survive much longer. After the oxygen ran a little lower, they might be able to get an extra hour from the remaining perox-ide—broken apart into steam and oxygen—which would be pretty horrible here in the cave, but it would give them a few more minutes. Then . . .

"Aren't you afraid?" he asked Ramachundra.

The little man smiled softly. "Of course, Mr. Hal-pern. Yes, I am afraid. But it is out of my hands. I am glad to have lived and to have seen this. I would rather think of that than fear now. And you?"

Fred wasn't sure. He'd been living with a growing fear from the moment they had realized the Station had plotted the location incorrectly; now it seemed curiously unreal. Maybe he was being fatalistic, too, since there was nothing anyone could do about it.

"I am writing my decision—my vote, you might say," Ramachundra said. "If they do not reach us in time, I wish my colleagues at the World Congress to know and to act. I think they will be very glad to do so. Because I have decided that we must do all we can to help this world, to build a colony here, and to make this a world-nation for all the peoples back there."

While Fred stared at him he squatted and picked up the pad again, signing his name with a flourish.

"It surprises you, no? Ah, yes. And you people sur-prise me. So much violence. Yet I see you sit patiently before a little plant, giving it a few last moments of exis-tence. That was a beautiful thing to do, my young friend. And I see you and your violent Major Wickman go out to do a violent thing with warm hearts and no hatred. I think—yes, I am sure—that I am beginning to see there are many kinds of violence. It is a new thought to me that sometimes accepting things as they are can be evil and that violence, when it hurts no other man, can be good. I have seen that it has not hurt you. I am very fond of you, Mr. Halpern. Very, yes. I would be proud to have you for a son. A world which does this cannot be a bad world for any people. So I have decided."

Fred felt touched and a little embarrassed. He finished his food under the old man's understanding smile.

Ramachundra broke the silence. "The World Congress can do a great deal for the Moon, I think. If the ship out there cannot be repaired, it does not matter. We will replace it for your government and there will be other ships we can buy. I have recommended that efforts be made to obtain and send a uranium power reactor as soon as is feasible. Oh, we can do much here. I am sure we will. Yes, we will."

Everything was going to be just wonderful, Fred thought, and a little bitterness crept into his mind. With the discovery of life here, the approval of the World Congress, plenty of power, and even a ship of their own, the colonists would be sure of their future, provided this cave was ever found.

Unless help came in four hours at the most, it would do none of the three here any good. He had very little idea of what he could do, beyond the peroxide, but he had to try something.

There was a little oxygen in the suit tank; and he began getting into the spacesuit to see what he could do about draining off the tractor fuel. The chemicals used to keep the air clean of water and carbon-dioxide were still working, and they should be able to handle the steam from the peroxide breakdown. Even an hour extra might make a difference.

He stepped through the lock and headed for the tractor. Then he stopped, frozen in his tracks. Words were pouring out of his phones, words in the voice of Dr. Sessions.

"Halpern. Wickman. Ramachundra. Fred, are you . . ."

"All here!" Fred choked out, his words thick in his own ears.

"Thank God! We were afraid . . . We'll be there in ten minutes. We can see your light from where we are. Hang on!"

Fred spun about to dash back into the cave and tell the others.

Twenty minutes later, they were sitting in the dormitory trailer, telling their stories and listening to the rescue account while Erica Neufeld hovered over them, trying to force more food and coffee on them. Only Villiers was missing. He'd gone to look at what remained of the plants Fred had found, and to fondle the bottle of spores and dream of new tests for the basic facts of life, protoplasm and cell structure.

The Station had been notified. Fred's father had not returned from the Earth where he'd been facing his old enemies, but there was a message, relayed from the Station:

"We have both won. Proud of you, Fred. Hope to see you soon."

Fred gazed at it again, and slowly pulled his mind back to the account of the trip as it was being told. Sessions and Gantry had realized that the Station had been wrong again, and decided to scout between that area and the one Fred suggested. Then, when the message came telling of the flash of light, they had doubled their speed to rescue the three men. The way had turned out to be one of the worst they had encountered; it was pockmarked with tiny craters, and the tractors had been forced to crawl cautiously. They hadn't known until Fred answered the call whether they would arrive in time.

Dr. Sessions stood up and motioned to Governor Gantry. The two men headed for the air lock, supposedly to plan the long trips back to their normal work. Sessions dropped a hand on Fred's shoulder as he passed. "I'd like to see you in the second tractor, Fred," he said quietly.

Fred nodded, glancing down at the telegram from his father again. "See you soon," he read. Maybe too soon. It would be nice to see his father, but not because he was kicked off the Moon. Sure, he was probably a hero again. He'd been that once before, and he knew how little it meant to the men who had to build the new world out of hard work and daily courage, not out of feats that simply made them heroes.

He finished his drink and stood up. There was a fresh bottle of oxygen on the suit now. That was one worry he no longer had.

He was disappointed to find both Gantry and Sessions in the tractor, going over the final details of the best routes. He'd hoped that he would have only the scientist to face. It was too late to back out now.

Sessions motioned him toward a seat, staring at him thoughtfully. The man's face was unreadable. Finally, Sessions shook his head. "All right, Fred, what do you think I should do with you?"

"Send me back to Earth, I suppose," Fred said. "I don't think you could execute me now, sir, in spite of your threat. But kicking me out is a pretty good substitute."

Sessions grinned briefly. "You've got an escape clause on that mutiny, you know. I remembered it after you pulled out."

Fred couldn't remember anything. He stared blankly at the other.

"I told you to use your own judgment, as I remember it," Sessions reminded him. "I suppose that entitled you to do anything you chose."

Fred considered it and rejected it. "No, sir. I knew perfectly well you meant I was to use my judgment by not running off. I was aware I was guilty of what you call mutiny when I left."

There was a sound that seemed to be an approving one from Gantry; Fred couldn't take his eyes from the face of the geologist.

Sessions sat playing with a pencil, apparently weighing every factor in his mind. Then he shrugged. "I'm not saying I'm not glad you disobeyed me, Fred. I'm the winner in this, too. I've already had more offers for funds than I ever thought there could be. Earth is waking up, particularly since the discovery of life here. The ships at Base will take off as soon as possible to return to the Station for more men and supplies. I'm as much a winner from your actions as Governor Gantry is. But I'm not considering that now. This is between you and me. Okay?"

"I expected it to be," Fred agreed. But he wondered to himself. Had he truly believed he could be condemned for succeeding?

"Fine. Then we've got the question of what to do about a man who disobeys his leader. Balanced against that, the problem of what to do about a leader who gives an impossible order." He nodded to himself. "Because I guess I always knew the order was one you couldn't obey, Fred. That's something no man has a right to expect—impossible obedience."

Gantry chuckled. "You've got yourself a nice problem," he said.

Sessions agreed. "Too nice a one, I'm afraid. It doesn't really matter who is responsible any more. I've been on exploring trips where a man under the leader turned into a hero. It doesn't work. It divides the loyalty of the men. They'll always feel that in the big moment it was Fred who was proved right and I who made a mistake. That's not good for morale. So, Fred, I can't take you back with me. I'd like to, but it wouldn't be wise, at least for a while."

He stood up. He held out a hand for one of the warmest clasps Fred had ever felt. "I wish I had a son like you," he said. "We'll see a lot of each other someday. I'll see to that."

Then he clumped out of the tractor before Fred could think of anything to say. He sat back, slowly aware that Gantry was watching him. The Governor reached out a large, work-toughened hand and rested it briefly on the young man's shoulder.

"Sessions is a hard man in some ways," he said, almost apologetically. "Maybe he's right, maybe not, but he has to do what he thinks best. He thinks a lot of you, though."

Sure, Fred thought. Everybody thought well of him this year—Sessions, Ramachundra, even Wickman. That would help somewhat back on Earth, but it wouldn't be enough. He grinned wryly. "I seemed to be everyone's favorite son lately."

The Governor chuckled. Then he sobered.

"I can't afford the luxury of adopting sons, Fred. I've got a world here to build while the luck is running with me. For that I don't need favorite sons or heroes. I need the best man I can get to do the hard, day to day work. Men who can get results, however they manage it."

"I know it," Fred said. He stood up to go. He hadn't expected Gantry to suggest anything or to get sentimental, and for that he was grateful.

Gantry reached over again and pressed him back into the seat. "You're not understanding well right now, young man. I said I need men who can work and who get things done. Well, I've talked to Sessions, and I've seen some of the results. You're one of the men I want, Fred, if you're willing to join up with us in the colony."

He ripped a sheet of paper out of a notebook and began scribbling on it. "I guess we'd better be formal about things, if the World Congress is to take us in. Here, sign this if you want to become one of us."

Fred's hand shook on the pen. He never read the words, and he didn't care if it sold him into bondage for twenty years.

"But why?" he asked as Gantry put the paper away. "Why?"

For years, he'd been trying to find a way to become part of all this, and every effort had failed. Now, when he'd rebelled more than ever before, and when what he had done could be misunderstood as glory-hogging if anything could, he was suddenly given a chance.

Gantry leaned back, studying him as if trying to read his mind. The Governor shook his head doubtfully.

"It's hard to explain, Fred," he said at last. "Call it judgment. When you were a kid, you did things because you didn't think them out and see all the results. I don't think you were rebellious—just lacking in good judgment. Because you were able to get some results, even then, it took a long time to live down the reputation, even after you began to change. Now, though, you're different. You've learned to take discipline. You've also got the judgment to see the results of your actions and to know when you have to act on your own. Maybe it's because you've stopped thinking only of what you want and learned to think about what has to be done for everyone. I don't know. But I know when I see judgment in a man, and you've got it."

He turned back to his papers, dismissing Fred.

Fred began moving the few things he had acquired as his own from the cave and tractor into one of the worn machines Gantry had brought. He was nearly finished before someone bothered to tell him that Sessions had transferred his tractor to Gantry's group. Apparently everyone but he knew he was to be the driver on the way back to Base. Then, with his belongings back where they had been for so long, there was nothing for him to do.

He went outside. Sessions was getting his group together, ready for the long haul back through the pass Fred had discovered. Blasting a way over the little chasm would be no problem for a fully equipped group. Men and women passed him, saying good-by and wishing him luck. Even Mona Williams came up. Maybe she'd decided he was more computer than man, finally accepting him.

He moved away, out onto the surface beyond the group, where he could feel the Moon all around him and see the stars in space. It was partly his Moon now, and he wanted the feeling of it by himself for a few minutes before he rejoined the men going back to build the colony.

He was almost back to the tractor when he saw Wickman hobbling toward him. There was a warm, friendly smile on the man's face as he bent over to touch helmets with Fred.

"Come on, Moon-man," he said. "We're almost ready."

Fred laughed with Wickman, and they moved together toward the waiting colonists.

Available at your bookstore or use this coupon.

the year's best movie."
— TIME

...is the year's paperback sensation!

"I loved STAR WARS and so will you."
— Jack Kroll, NEWSWEEK

All the action and fascination of this most
spectacular space fantasy

PLUS 16 PAGES OF MOVIE STILLS IN COLOR!

A **DEL REY** BOOK published by **BB** BALLANTINE BOOKS

▼ Available at your local bookstore or mail the coupon below ▼